D1520102

RATTLESNAKE GULCH

RATTLESNAKE GULCH

•

Marjorie M. McGinley

AVALON BOOKS
THOMAS BOUREGY AND COMPANY, INC.
401 LAFAYETTE STREET
NEW YORK, NEW YORK 10003

Library of Congress Catalog Card Number: 98-96852
ISBN 0-8034-9341-X

All the characters in this book are fictitious,
and any resemblance to actual persons,
living or dead, is purely coincidental.

PRINTED IN THE UNITED STATES OF AMERICA
ON ACID-FREE PAPER
BY HADDON CRAFTSMEN, BLOOMSBURG, PENNSYLVANIA

I dedicate this book to my husband, Ernie

Chapter One

It was a gut feeling, more than anything. Every spring, one day some instinct would tell him it was the right day, *the* day, and every spring he would get on his horse and ride out there; it was something that had to be done.

Every year, since he had begun these solitary journeys, it had been all right. For three years, ever since he'd become sheriff, he had never missed. It was 1869 already. Time seemed to be rushing by.

This year was no different . . . at least so far. If Dan Turner had to explain how he knew the special day, he'd have to think a bit; maybe it was the way the sun looked in the sky, or maybe the temperature, or maybe it was the warm breeze striking his face a certain way. But always he knew.

His rich red-brown polished saddle creaked underneath the weight of his body and the faint scent of Sarah, his chestnut-colored horse, crept up to him as he rode toward the gulch.

Sometimes, in past years, he'd felt foolish making this expedition, year after year, but some vague feeling of being responsible—to protect people he didn't even know—made him continue his compulsory annual journey.

It took three hours traveling in a northeast direction to get there from town, and of course three hours to get back. He tended not to stay too long once he'd got there.

He had a different feeling about this year's journey that, so far, he'd been able to push back down where it belonged; it was just pure foolishness.

Still . . .

It was probably just nerves, he thought. It had been a tough winter—the snow over eighteen feet deep in many places up in the Sierras—and it had taken a long time to melt, filling the rivers and streams with a turbulent, dangerous runoff. In the distance, the higher mountains even further to the northeast still had their white caps of snow; some of those mountains were over ten thousand feet high.

Sarah's foot disturbed a rock, and it clattered down a few feet. He was a bit surprised. Perhaps she was sensing his mood. It was getting hillier and rockier. They both needed to pay attention to what they were doing.

He suddenly knew what it was.

Many settlers had arrived in the past year, and most of the best land had been claimed. New arrivals settled for poorer and poorer land. And the gulch . . . well, he just hoped some darn fool hadn't arrived late in the fall or early winter and built a cabin up here in this isolated area.

He berated himself for not coming out here sooner, but

he knew that he couldn't have; his mother had been dying, and he couldn't leave her.

Even for one day.

He had put her in her final resting place next to his father three days ago.

He'd found a peaceful place overlooking a valley on a meadowlike area of his property for his dad when he'd passed on, and now his parents were together. And he was alone.

Thirty-four years old last October 14.

He'd been busy catching up on work since then, things that had been put off while his mother had been painfully coughing—terrible wracking coughs—and wasting away.

Some were things that shouldn't have been put off, like this trip. Still, he was not sorry that he had spent the time with her before she died.

He still felt occasional sharp pangs of grief about her death. She'd been his last living relative. His brother during the War of the Rebellion, then his father, and now his mother, all dead. His brother's body had not been sent home, and he'd had to come back home to help out because his father had lost an arm fighting.

The sudden smell of woodsmoke jolted him out of his thoughts. He leaned forward and hurried Sarah with his knees, even though the rocky terrain did not warrant speed. She picked up the pace to just under that for roping a newborn calf.

He silently thanked her for being surefooted and dependable—a good partner. He patted her on the side of her shiny reddish brown neck, trusting her to choose the right path through the rocks.

They rode up and down a low rise and he realized he

had less than an eighth of a mile to go before he came to that last hilly rise of patches of weeds, rock, and scant grass that looked down into the gulch.

Two minutes later, he was looking down from that rise.

Fools!

He could see the unnamed silvery green stream that ran through the gulch, and just beyond that, set far too close to the water, stood a hastily built, poorly constructed cabin.

It was more of a shack or shanty than a cabin, built by a man with poor carpentry skills, to say the least. Crooked, shabby work. Only about ten by fourteen feet, the boards on the small building were trimmed unevenly and hammered together haphazardly.

And this past winter, the nights had been so cold! Someone must have stuffed rags or paper or mud in the cracks, he hoped. He couldn't see from here; it was too far away.

Behind the cabin was an area that backed up to the bottom of a craggy hill—really the bottom of a small steep mountain. There were piles of boulders close to the bottom of the steep incline.

A small innocent-looking black hole between two boulders was at the bottom of the largest pile, which faced directly east toward the morning sunrise. The sandy dirt in front of the boulders fanned out in a gentle downward slope, leveling out about twenty feet in back of the cabin.

The door to the cabin was open, facing the stream.

"Darn blasted fools!" he said to himself.

Even Easterners should have had enough brains to build further back from the stream because of water that came down from the mountains. Many a person had been washed away in the flooding waters of the Sierra snowmelt swelling and rushing down a stream or river. Right now this stream was innocently running wide, flat, shallow, and clear, so maybe they'd been lucky. Maybe most of the runoff had taken a different route, but streams would be gradually rising through July.

But there was much more immediate danger here.

As he looked, he saw a thin young woman with brown hair and a loose pale blue dress hanging laundry on scraggly bushes thirty feet to the left of the cabin. Behind her was a small, bedraggled-looking clump of cottonwood trees. A little yellow-haired girl about two years old played near her mother, putting pebbles and small rocks in lines on the ground.

Sarah snorted, cleaning the dust out of her nostrils, and the woman looked up at them. She showed no sign of alarm, only relief.

She stopped what she was doing, putting a small green child's dress back on the pile of wet items on the rocks closest to her.

He was too late.

As he watched, they began to crawl toward the woman and the girl, coming around both sides of the cabin from the back, and heading in all directions, many slithering directly toward the woman and child. *Hundreds of snakes, all kinds, but mostly western rattlers.*

Western rattlers were known for being nervous, bad tempered, and easily aroused. And along with the western diamondback, responsible for almost all the fatal snakebites he'd ever heard about—or seen.

She didn't see them. She was looking up the hill at him. They kept coming, silently. She had a totally inappropriate look of happiness on her face.

She waved.

The small child looked up and waved, too, copying her mother. He saw now that they wore matching blue dresses, and that the child's curly hair was such a pale, pale yellow that it was almost white.

In thirty seconds she and the child would be surrounded by rattlers and other snakes, coming out from their communal wintering-over place, out of the centuries-old underground cave under the pile of rocks on the slope behind the cabin.

He wasn't sure Sarah would go forward; she had more sense than most people. He couldn't take the chance, even though it would have been faster to get down the slope and reach them on horseback. Once down there, he didn't know what Sarah might do.

He jumped off Sarah, landed on the ground, and ran forward, down the hill. His sudden movement instantly changed the woman's friendly, welcoming attitude.

She watched him running toward her and she reached down and quickly scooped up her child, glancing frantically around trying to decide whether to head for the cabin—where, foolishly, her gun probably was—or to head for the cottonwood trees in back of her.

"Up where the cabin really ought to be," he thought incongruously to himself as he ran, "if there weren't so dang many rattlers here."

Rattlers who had been out for a while already, quietly warming themselves behind the shack in the morning sun, while she'd gone unknowingly about her chores.

Western rattlers—with the ability to change their color to blend in perfectly with the background within one to two minutes.

To become almost invisible to anybody or anything not paying attention.

Still running, he reached the flat section of dirt on his side of the stream and then strode through the green water as fast as he could, coming out on the other side—not stopping to think about how close the snakes would be to his feet as he rushed toward her.

Never a talkative man in the best of times, he managed to hiss out a quiet warning, ''Snakes!'' between his teeth as he ran. She looked down, seeing them for the first time—in horror—and at the same time struggling with the child squirming in her arms, who was futilely trying to get out of her mother's tight grip and back to playing with her rocks.

He let his instincts choose a path through the first oncoming, wriggling snakes, hoping that the child's squawks of annoyance—growing louder by the second—wouldn't 'rouse the rattlers. Or that his running wouldn't trigger some primeval alarm, even in their newly awakened state.

''Snakes, I mean you no harm,'' he said silently to them, hoping that they might understand in some mysterious, mystical way. ''Just let us get the heck out of here,'' he said silently to them in his thoughts.

Snakes, snakes, and more snakes!

He reached her at the very second that she had decided to run forward toward him, and they crashed together. With his elbow, he could feel her rib bones as they hit. He had almost knocked her down, but he quickly reached up and around and grabbed her arm to restore her balance, and she came upright again.

Recovering quickly, they turned and made a run for it, him grabbing the baby from her as they ran close together like a team—she was on his right—heading toward the stream.

He was in less danger than she was, because she looked like she was wearing only Eastern-style thin black leather shoes that came only an inch or two above her ankles. He could only hope that a snake would strike her full skirt instead of her legs. He had on his brown leather cowboy boots, which came up to about three inches below his knees, but he'd known of rattlers that could strike as high as a man's thighs.

They splashed through the stream and ran up the slope, reaching Sarah, who was waiting nervously at the top of the hill. Her brown eyes were wild and rolling and she was prancing skittishly. She was ready to bolt, but his sweetheart of a horse had stayed.

"Good girl, Sarah," he said to her.

The woman's chest was heaving in and out from running, and he could see she was painfully thin. He could see her rib bones through the thin blue material of her dress as she breathed. The skirt of her pale blue dress was wet all around about a foot up from the bottom, making it a darker blue. She reached down to squeeze a little of the dripping water out of the material.

When she finished about a minute later, she stood up straight, and he saw that her hands were trembling quite a bit. But he was not about to be kind after what she had put him through.

"Dangit, you stupid people built in Rattlesnake Gulch!" he said loudly and angrily.

She was quiet.

She didn't answer but a different expression came on her face, maybe one of anguish or maybe feeling sorry for herself and her child. She just lowered her head toward her chest so he couldn't see her face and began to cry silently.

Seeing that, the child also began to cry, and cry a lot louder than the mother—a loud whaahing noise coming from about three inches from his left ear as he held her in his arms.

The noise went right into his ear.

He wasn't used to holding youngsters, anyway.

Here they were, the three of them—the four of them, counting Sarah—standing at the top of the rise; snakes down below; one angry man yelling and two crying females. One very little one crying very loud.

Dang!

Now what?

His presence had calmed Sarah down considerably, so he thought a few seconds and then reached up and gently put the crying, squirming, child on Sarah's saddle, suddenly afraid he would drop the girl. Her dress had a wide neck and was so loose that he was afraid she'd slide right out of it onto the ground. She was even thinner than he'd thought. He felt her tiny bones through the dress as he held her in the saddle until she seemed steady on it.

Suddenly, he felt awfully sorry for her.

They must have been starving!

Now he was sorry that this tiny, frail child had heard him yell at her mother. He began to feel ashamed of himself and terribly guilty.

Tiny as the little girl was, she turned, looked directly into his eyes and sized him up.

Miraculously, she stopped crying.

"Horsey," she said. "Horsey!"

The woman looked at him, fear still on her face.

"Can snakes swim?" she asked.

"Most snakes are good swimmers," he said shortly. "Some like it less than others," he added. He didn't mention that even when swimming, rattlers can deliver a deadly bite; or that after storing up their venom all winter, their bite would be especially deadly right now. She didn't need to know all that right this minute. . . .

The snakes hadn't crossed the stream yet—Sarah would have notified him if they had—but they had to hurry. He also had to ask her a few things, quick, before they could leave. Because of the child, he made an effort to change his usually deep voice to a softer pitch.

"Where is your husband?" he asked stiffly, at the same time turning Sarah around by leading her by her bridle to face the direction of town.

When Sarah was turned around he continued walking the horse with the child on the saddle away from the snakes as he spoke; one hand steadying the child on the saddle and the other hand on the bridle, not waiting for the woman's answer.

The woman followed closely as he went, unspeaking, but seemingly in silent agreement that additional distance from the snakes was a good idea before too much else was said.

When they were safely over the rise, he stopped.

The woman was quiet for a moment, but he could see she was trying to say something difficult.

"Dead." she said, finally. "Fever. Fever and ague. Died. November."

The ague—violent recurring shivering and sharp chills. He could vividly picture it in his mind. He had seen it before.

It was his turn to be silent, taking in her situation. But he was still angry at her husband.

"You alone all winter?"

She looked down at the ground as she began walking again. He thought she was probably crying again.

"Yes."

He wasn't sorry for the durn fool, he didn't think that it was a great loss to the world. But perhaps she had thought her husband was wonderful, so he said gruffly, "Sorry."

She looked up at him. She accepted this without comment or without changing her facial expression, which he couldn't quite read. Chagrin or embarrassment? Sorrow?

Quickly he said, "You two all alone out here?"

She nodded yes.

"Anyone else back down there in the cabin?"

She nodded no.

"No horse?"

She shook her head.

"No mules, no livestock?"

No cows, no mules, no oxen, no barn. Not even chickens.

She had nodded no to everything.

They had nothing!

She'd had to bury her husband herself, she said. And she had had to finish nailing the final boards on the shack. That explained a lot about the construction.

"You're the first person I've seen, since November, with the exception of my daughter here," she added.

She'd been courageous, he had to give her that.

"I'll take you to town," he said a little less roughly.

He thought about the cabin in back of them and knew that there would be no chance of retrieving anything from there. At least, not now.

For the first time he noticed that the woman was short. He was probably a foot taller than she was.

He was relieved that they were safe.

He nodded his head toward the saddle, indicating that it was time for her to get up and ride behind the little girl.

The woman indicated that she would accept his help getting up into the saddle of his tall horse, by putting out her hand to grab his shoulder and raising her foot. He cupped his hands together so she could step up. The stirrup was too high for her to step up into, and he didn't want to take the time to adjust it right this minute.

He had an urgent feeling that the evil-looking pitted heads of rattlers might glide silently over the top of the rise any moment.

She put her small black shoe into his cupped hands, straightened her leg and was up and over the saddle, sliding behind the child, adjusting her wet skirt quickly and modestly as best she could; this was not a woman's sidesaddle, and she did not have on a divided skirt. He politely looked away until her skirts were all set, and she had adjusted herself on the saddle.

They set out, going southwest toward town, down out of this area of steep foothills.

He felt guilty and sorry. Perhaps he was getting too harsh with people. He was getting too used to dealing with those who broke the law. He'd forgotten how to be kind to regular people outside of his own family.

He walked alongside Sarah, as they went back the way he had come, still holding the bridle, still keeping an eye out for snakes, to the place past the rise where he had begun smelling woodsmoke. Then he stopped briefly and shortened the stirrups for the woman. He thought for a moment, then he pulled four sticks of beef jerky out of his saddlebag and silently handed two to each of them. As he closed up the saddlebag he reflected on the great amount of food in his house, with hardly anyone to eat it. And the two of them had spent the winter close to starving.

In a little while, he'd give them something more to eat, but right now, they needed to put some distance between themselves and that shack and get the heck out of this whole area.

The woman was looking at him expectantly to see if he was going to swing up behind her on the horse now, but he couldn't do that to Sarah. He was a hundred and eighty pounds by himself. He handed the reins to the woman.

She nodded, understanding, and squeezed her legs gently to get Sarah to only go slowly. But she was also obviously eager to put some miles between herself and her child and that shack, same as he was.

He sighed, and began walking alongside them, close to Sarah's head, although he had let go of the bridle. It would be a long hike back to town. The woman probably didn't weigh much over one hundred pounds, the child less than twenty, he guessed. Sarah didn't know it yet, but she was getting a break on this deal.

The woman politely kept Sarah moving at the slow pace, so he could keep up.

After a few minutes, he saw that the woman was an able horsewoman, so he moved off, further away from Sarah—between eight and ten feet from them—to give both Sarah and himself a bit more room for walking.

He didn't see much need for more talk, but the woman obviously did.

Formally she said, "My name is Cassie Chadwick, and

this here's Moira.'' She nodded, indicating the child riding on the saddle in front of her.

She had her left hand on the reins and her right arm around Moira, in front of her.

''Dan Turner,'' he said.

She made a point of looking at the badge on his leather vest.

He looked down and glanced at where she was looking—the brown leather vest with the badge pinned above the left-hand side pocket, over his heart. Then he glanced at the rest of himself. Under the vest he had on his light brown shirt. Below that, he had on black whipcord pants and his brown boots. Ordinary clothing.

She looked at him long and hard.

''You sheriff of Little Sage, or River Grove?''

She was referring to the fact that the people of Little Sage, finally realizing that Sage had two meanings, had recently changed its name officially to River Grove.

He tended to still call it Little Sage, the name it had been since he'd moved there and up until a year ago.

He nodded, then said, ''Yes.''

''Is that where we're going?'' she asked.

He nodded again.

Sarah plodded along.

The boots he had on had high heels that were made for riding and for safely keeping your bootheels in the stirrups. Walking long distances in them was not the most pleasant thing in the world, especially on this rolling terrain. He'd probably have blisters when he got back to town.

No one spoke for half an hour, except Moira, who was happily talking baby talk to herself and the ''Horsey,'' unaware of the tension between the two grown-ups.

Finally Cassie spoke again.

"Why wasn't there a sign?" she asked. "There could have been a sign: 'Rattlesnake Gulch,' or 'Beware of Rattlesnakes.' "

He thought for a moment. It was a good question. It interrupted his thinking about what to do with her.

He'd been thinking that maybe Julia Anderson would take them in, temporarily. She was a widow, and a real nice person and he guessed she might be lonely sometimes.

"Nobody much around here can read or write," he said, finally.

"I can," she said, making him realize he had just sounded like a fool. Sometimes he forgot how modern people and things were getting to be. It was true that more and more people could read and write these days. He could, himself.

Not speaking much after that, they continued traveling southwest toward the town.

An hour later they stopped to give Sarah a drink from a stream tumbling down from the mountains before they crossed it. The woman and child got down off the horse. First she handed him the child, and then she got down. Sarah stepped up to the water to drink as Dan gave his full canteen to the woman and she gave the girl, Moira, a drink before taking a drink herself. When she handed it back, he took a drink, and then refilled it in the stream, and capped it.

While they were there, he pulled some thick slices of ham on large crumbly biscuits, which he had brought for lunch, out of his saddlebags and passed one each to the woman and child. He tried not to watch as they ate, but he could see that they ate hungrily and seemed grateful for the food. The little girl, Moira, was saying ''Um-um,'' as she chewed, as if it was the best food she'd ever eaten.

Sarah was happily eating the grass that grew on the banks of the stream.

They each drank some more, and then he refilled the canteen again. Cassie washed her hands and Moira's in the cold, clear, bubbly stream, then she remounted, and he handed Moira up to her.

They set off again.

It was a long walk.

The child was being remarkably good, happily riding along on Sarah's saddle in front of her mother.

Most of the rest of the way they were quiet. Pretty much the only sound was the thud of Sarah's feet, and that of his own boots. He was thinking about her and the child and what was to become of them. Also about things that he was worried about back in Little Sage.

And about how his feet hurt. And about how he might have had a little girl this age if Maryellen had not given up waiting for him during the war and gone off and married Terrance Youngblood. . . .

Chapter Two

It was getting close to dark when they reached the meadow near the edge of town where his three-room ranch house made of wide, white-painted vertical planks stood. Inside, there was a big kitchen and two small bedrooms. In the kitchen was one of the latest models of iron stoves that he had bought for his mother a year ago, before she took sick.

For the last few days he had lived there alone for the first time since his return to Little Sage, a little over three years ago.

It was almost too dark to see the fine grass for grazing, and the purple, orange, and yellow wildflowers that bloomed now in the back of his house near his corral, and the small, spring-fed pond he was so lucky to have on his property in back of the barn.

The night his mother died, he had seen a fine reddish

buck with a huge rack of antlers drinking from the pond. They'd looked at each other for a few seconds before the buck bounded away. A magnificent sight on a terribly sad day.

A canyon area north of the town gave way to a view of distant peaks beyond the visible foothills, some of them pine covered. There were shrubs closer by near the edge of the meadow. In the distance a mountain that was over four thousand feet high rose to the east of the town.

The town of Little Sage—River Grove—sat along the edge of the foothills of the Sierras. It got its new name from the cottonwood groves that grew along both sides of the stream that ran along the south side of town.

All the streams in this area basically ran west, off the Sierra Nevada Mountains, toward the Sacramento River.

In the fall, bright yellow leaves from the cottonwoods floated like colorful little boats down the stream. Dan thought that the little girl would probably like seeing that. She liked rocks and horses, so she'd probably like the pretty yellow leaves—if she was still around in the fall.

The town itself ran in a short direct line from east to west out in a wide valley in the foothills, following the general path of the river.

During the great mining years, and even now, the town of River Grove was mainly a supply place—now mostly for people traveling either up into the Sierras, going further west to the coast, or north or south. There were a few ranchers and older farmers. And more and more, there were homesteaders from the East—new farmers—and more cattle ranchers moving up from the southern part of the state.

Unfortunately, its location also gave an occasional stranger passing through what they each thought was the unique idea that if they robbed, they could easily escape up into the mountains to get away; and so his job as sheriff kept him busy.

The locals had a name for it, they called it "heading for the tall timber"—that meant skedaddling high up where, supposedly, people can't find you. The criminals all thought that they could "hide out" a few days up there and then go on their way with their loot. But the steep mountains behind Little Sage held a few surprises for the foolish, the unwary, and the unobservant.

The irony was that he knew all the trails up into the Sierras—including the shortcuts—as well, or better than they did. He was familiar with the local mountains while many—actually most—of the crooks were people passing through for the first time, heading east, west, north or south.

Dan loved the mountains and was used to them; he respected them.

Some of the lawbreakers didn't respect them anymore than they respected anybody or anything else.

The view east from town, which Daniel Turner loved the best, was a view of these familiar mountains.

In midsummer, the snowcap of the largest mountain in sight melted in the form of a large Y because of the formation of the rocks. It varied in shape from time to time and from year to year, but locals called it the Big Y, also meaning as a joke the Big Why?—as in why would anyone go up there? It was tall, steep, and dangerous in spots.

Some of the other mountains had more gradual slopes and were easier to climb.

The view west from town was of the valley, which was far from level in this area. Small hills—mounds really—covered with brush and some oaks dotted the area.

They came to the road that led to the town, coming down to join it from the northeast, and, gratefully, Dan followed Sarah as she began following it west toward town.

His first order of business was to get these two females to Mrs. Anderson's house before it became so late in the evening that a knock on the door would alarm the widow. Julia Anderson had a good heart; he was sure that the two would be welcomed.

They went west through town past Ferd Cody's general store, past a saloon, Dan's sheriff's office, the livery stable across the street, more saloons, restaurants, a vacant building, the blacksmith shop past the King Bank, the land office, and finally to the west end, near the churches, where there was a cluster of homes.

Saying, "Wait here a minute," to Cassie, Moira, and Sarah, he opened the gate of the little white picket fence that Mr. Anderson had painstakingly built for Mrs. Anderson before his death five years ago. It could use a new coat of paint, he noticed. Dan went inside the yard on the left side of the street, carefully closing the little gate behind him, and went up on the porch and knocked on Mrs. Anderson's front door.

Showing good manners, Cassie and Moira waited, still sitting up on the horse's back.

He stood back from the door, and took off his hat so that she could see who it was without being frightened.

"Why Sheriff Turner. What brings you here?" Mrs. Anderson said in a very friendly way, as she timidly opened the door a crack before opening it wide when she saw who it was.

She came out on the porch.

Julia Anderson, at about five foot five, was only six

inches shorter than he was. Her neat brown hair was parted in the middle and drawn back into a bun. She had a pretty face and long eyelashes that slightly curled up.

"I don't want to impose, but I got two ladies out here needing some assistance, and, hopefully, a place to spend the night," he said. "They seem like nice people," he added softly.

Julia Anderson waved them in with one arm, using the other arm to put her hand over her eyebrows to shield her eyes so that she might see better in the dusk on the porch.

"Come on in, folks," she said loudly.

Together he and Mrs. Anderson walked off the porch, and out through the small yard and back out to the gate; and he could see Mrs. Anderson's usual prim and proper reserve melt as she saw little Moira.

Dan threw Sarah's reins lightly over the closest picket on the fence and made introductions all around.

"Well, come on in," Mrs. Anderson repeated warmly, as she watched Cassie hand Moira to Dan and then dismount.

He handed Moira back to Cassie.

"Come on in and make yourself to home," Mrs. Anderson was saying, as they walked through the gate again and up the path to the door.

Julia Anderson looked back when they reached the porch.

"You comin?" Mrs. Anderson asked Dan, but he shook his head no.

"I'll be over to check on them in the morning," Dan said, as he finally swung back up on Sarah for the last short trip back through town to home.

As usual since Mr. Anderson's death, Mrs. Anderson

was dressed all in black. She'd started wearing it as the proper sign of mourning, and then decided she liked it. She'd never changed back to wearing any other colors once the mourning period—for her a year—was up.

Some of the town ladies had tried to get her to wear at least a dark blue, but she was adamant on keeping to the black. It had been five years now, if he counted right. Her husband had died while Dan was gone.

But lately, he'd noticed she'd been adding white lace trim to the ends of the sleeves and around her collar.

Chapter Three

Dan dismounted in front of his barn, opened the door, and brought Sarah inside.

He took down the oil lamp that was hanging on a hook, lit it, and then put it back on the hook. Then he gave Sarah a drink and some oats, and brushed her.

"You were a good girl today, Sarah," he said as he brushed. She turned her head to look back at him; he was brushing near her withers. Sometimes, he could swear that Sarah understood everything he said.

He took care of the other stock, and threw feed—crushed corn kernels—to the chickens in the little chicken coop in the back of the barn.

Finishing, he went back into the barn, blew out the lamp, hung it back up, closed the door of the barn, and went into the house.

Pulling off his boots, he walked in his stocking feet to the iron stove and lit a fire. Nights got cold.

And his feet really hurt.

He went to the bucket and got some water and put it on to heat in the big kettle. Some coffee would be good about now, he thought.

After he had eaten some more of the ham and some bread with his coffee, and cleaned up his supper dishes, he went and sat down at the large sturdy oak rectangular table that was in the center of the kitchen.

He got a basin, poured some of the warm water into it, pulled off his socks, slid the basin underneath the table and put his feet into the basin with an ''aah.''

Sitting at the table, with his feet still in the basin, he put his head in his hands.

Just before reaching town, Cassie had said one more thing. He knew she was trying to thank him, and praise him, and be polite. She'd said, ''You look like a man that does what needs to be done . . . and does it without complaint.'' She looked at him and continued, ''And you're a strong, solid man.''

She'd turned to look at him when she said that.

''And Moira and I thank you for what you did for us today.''

To be polite, he murmured, ''It's nothing.''

''No, it's *not* nothing,'' she said forcefully. ''It's *a lot* to me and Moira . . . you saved our lives.''

She didn't say whether she meant from starvation, or from the snakes.

Maybe she meant both.

It didn't matter.

Then she'd looked at him almost bitterly and said,

"Doesn't anything ever bother you?" He thought she meant his stiffness in dealing with her. It was not something he could answer.

Of course he hadn't told her how his feet hurt. And how he hated rattlers. Or about the war. Or about Maryellen.

Perhaps she wasn't asking him to really answer, because she turned her head and resumed looking forward over Sarah's head as she rode.

He never told anyone his weaknesses and fears; you never let on to anyone any of your weaknesses if you were the sheriff—someone would take advantage of it. Not that he'd ever told anyone, even when he was a boy.

Not even his mother or father. You just didn't do that in his family. It was never discussed.

But it was kind of a lonely thing.

He still missed Maryellen sometimes. He'd tried to work up hate for her, to get her out of his mind, but he couldn't. He couldn't really blame her for not waiting. Not for three long years of war.

She'd been so warm, and friendly, it was no wonder that Youngblood had come along and courted her in his absence. She'd had a pretty face and bouncy brown curly hair.

She'd always said that she liked his blue eyes and black hair, and she'd said she hoped that their babies would look like him.

Now there would be no babies. She lived in Sacramento with her husband and their daughter.

Pastor Cook kept telling him that the man who delivered potatoes to Ferd's store had a beautiful daughter, and that Dan ought to take a look-see. But so far, he'd never seen her. He didn't think that any other woman could hold a candle to Maryellen. . . .

Chapter Four

The next morning at eight, he checked his office, and things seemed to be quiet for the moment. He'd been up since dawn caring for his livestock and farm animals.

Around ten o'clock he rode Sarah over to Mrs. Anderson's little white house to check on how they all were doing. In fact, the two women were standing at the "good" dining-room table in Mrs. Anderson's parlor—used only for company—and were busy cutting out new dresses for Cassie and Moira from cheerful green, yellow, and white calico.

Dan guessed that since Cassie had no money, Mrs. Anderson had paid for it. Thread and needles were on the table, close to a little red pincushion covered with pins.

The pure white lace tablecloth that was usually on the table was folded neatly on one of the fancy wooden chairs near the front window, leaving the wood of the table exposed so that the women could lay out the material on it.

He didn't know how women did it; a woman's dress had so many parts to sew together.

Moira was sitting on the floor playing happily with Mrs. Anderson's pots and pans.

Mrs. Anderson said that Cassie and Moira were all right staying there for a few days, so Dan rode back on over to the sheriff's office.

Back to everyday problems.

He was thinking about these problems as he rode through town from Julia Anderson's house up the street past the businesses, two of the saloons, and then to his office.

Handily, his office was placed near the four saloons: It cut down on a lot of shenanigans knowing the sheriff was a couple of steps away.

He tried to keep on top of things.

But someone was stealing Burt Black's chickens.

And the town ladies were after him about Alister, again.

Halfway up the second mountain to the left of the Big Y—one of the middle-height mountains that the locals called Grizzly Butte—an old hermit-prospector lived. His name was Alister Skinner. He was seldom seen. Up there, he lived all alone.

Sometimes Dan envied him. Alister had survived up there alone all these years by being observant, careful, and self-reliant.

Dan knew a bit about where Alister lived from local gossip.

Alister had found a high meadow area in which to build his cabin, Dan had heard. He lived alone up there in the peace and quiet, along with very hard winters and deep snow.

He was a walking kind of mountain man; he had no horse, at least none that Dan knew of. That alone would have made it difficult for him to get up and down the mountain simply to steal chickens. He'd never been down to town that Dan knew of; he got his ammunition and food supplies—if he bought any—from some other source.

In a way, Dan envied the old mountain man: In spring, Alister saw masses of beautiful mountain flowers, and, on the lower meadowlike slopes, thick grasses.

There was a rumor that Alister lived up there because many years ago he had scalped his mistress. Harvey King, the banker, told that story to anyone who would listen, and had been telling it for many years, whenever the subject of Alister came up.

Alister had been up there for many years now, and had never bothered anybody that Dan had heard of. In fact, he had fed or rescued a few people foolhardy enough to be caught "up mountain" in unexpectedly bad weather. Winter storms came up suddenly in the mountains and often lasted a long time. They also might come upon you suddenly in the springtime when you thought snowstorms were over.

But a few busybody town ladies were insisting that it was Alister who was sneaking around the edge of town and that he was the one who had stolen some of the Black family's chickens.

Dan supposed he'd have to go up there and check on Alister. Perhaps the old man had become too weak and old to hunt for food and so was desperate enough to be raiding chicken coops at night.

He got down off Sarah and unlocked his office and went inside. There was a desk situated so he could look out the window, on the right as he entered the door, and two cells in the far back.

To the right of the two small cells in the back of the room was a small room which led to a back door. Also in the back room was a cot, and some of his supplies and clothing. Sometimes on Saturday nights he slept in town, but he hadn't since his mother had gotten so ill.

There was also a spare cot in the front room on the left wall where his part-time helper, Jay Garrity, sometimes slept when he was on overnight duty. On the wall in back of the desk was a gun rack, high up, out of the reach of children. The guns were well cared for.

He had barely taken off his hat when there was a rapid couple of knocks on the door, and Mrs. Nedlinger appeared, very upset—almost distraught.

''Sheriff, you've got to help me,'' she said. The spry little old woman, probably sixty if she was a day, came in, shut the door behind her (most proper women left the door open if they were in the room with a man not their immediate relative or husband), and sat down in the chair facing his desk. This was a rare thing for her, showing him exactly how upset she was. She usually stood to scold people or to do business.

She motioned for him to sit down at his desk. This was official business, he saw.

He sat, after hanging his brown hat on a hook near the door.

He chuckled inwardly, sure her problem was a small one. Nobody took on Mrs. Nedlinger if they didn't have to. She was a town force to be reckoned with.

But here she was, all distraught and shutting herself in with him in private.

''Nellie, what are you doing,'' he joked, ''shutting the door like that? You want people to say I'm courting you or we're doing something improper? You want your church ladies to talk about us?''

''Daniel Jefferson Turner, you young whippersnapper, you mind yourself.''

Then she added gently, ''You mind your manners,'' softening just a bit. ''I'll get right to the point.''

She always did, he thought to himself, inwardly smiling.

He nodded.

She wiggled to get more comfortable in the hard oak chair, the full skirts of her gray dress leaving nothing but the tiniest tip of black shiny shoes showing. Her black purse was neatly held on her lap, and her black shawl wrapped around her shoulders. She sat up very straight, her lips pursed with worry.

He'd very rarely seen her without her mentioning at least once that she was cold. She spoiled almost every social event he attended—and she never missed one if she could help it—by constantly complaining she was cold.

In fact, she was a complainer by nature, he thought.

This time, however, it was obvious that it was not a frivolous complaint she was here for. By her attitude, he guessed she had a real one.

''Three of my goats are missing.''

Local women who had trouble nursing babies, and infants whose mothers had died in childbirth, depended upon Mrs. Nedlinger's goats. The goat milk was strained through cloth, watered down, and warmed and fed to babies using little glass bottles with rubber nipples. For three goats to be missing, therefore, was a serious thing.

"Three goats went missing, over a period of a couple of weeks. It ain't a varmint, neither, 'lest a varmint these days has learned to open and close pen doors and latches," Mrs. Nedlinger added.

She meant that it wasn't a wild creature that had taken her livestock; if she had thought that, she would have gone to the Wolf Committee, the local group that went after predators of the four-legged kind that preyed on anyone's livestock in the local area. And sometimes, they tracked a grizzly that had gone after a steer outside of town.

"Comes when my back is turned, opens the gate and walks off with one goat at a time."

Dan thought for a moment.

"Who have you told about this?"

"You."

"No one else?"

She harrumphed, making a derogatory noise with her mouth and nose, and then said, "What, do you think I go and advertise my troubles around town before coming here?"

Again he almost chuckled.

Usually it was Mrs. Nedlinger who was the trouble in town. It was Mrs. Nedlinger who was the head and leader of the Anti-Alister Group, as he secretly called them in his head.

And Mrs. Nedlinger's culinary "specialty" was making huge sourdough pretzels. She forced them on every guest she had. They were so hard they'd break your teeth, if you weren't careful.

Some people went so far as to say that she made pretzels

only because they were cheap—made only with salt, flour, and water and not much else. That way, she didn't have to spend money on any fancier vittles to feed visitors—that is, if she should have any. Knowing about her pretzel fetish, she had very few, as far as Dan knew.

That way, she had more money to put in Harvey King's bank, people said.

Some people in town would probably jokingly say that the goats had run away to get away from being fed Mrs. Nedlinger's stale pretzels. But Dan wasn't so sure if telling about the thefts was a good idea, after he followed her back to her small ranch house across the road—and back off the main road by a half mile—from his own home. She was, in effect, one of his closest neighbors.

He examined the pen where the goats "went missing" as Mrs. Nedlinger called it, and found, as he suspected, that any tracks had been blown away by the wind.

The soil was so dry and dusty that in dry weather small puffs of dirt arose with every step. It was also the kind that made the worst kind of drippy mud—the mud that liked to slide down hills when it was wet. Mud that turned into puddinglike consistency.

Because it was a silent type of crime, and goats that suddenly turned up in a neighbor's yard were sure to be recognized and spotted, he had an idea.

"We'll keep this theft quiet for a few days while I look around," he said to her. "Can you keep this quiet—not tell anyone?"

She looked at him, alarmed for a few seconds until she thought it over.

Keep Mrs. Nedlinger quiet?

Gossipy Mrs. Nedlinger? Quiet?

Her eyes widened almost in alarm at the thought of keeping this juicy bit quiet. None of her friends speculating with her as to who had done it? It was almost an outrageous thought.

Then she thought of Daisy, Freida, and Marigold, her goats. Her missing goats.

Yes, she'd do anything. Anything it took.

Firmly, forcefully, she nodded.

''You make darn sure you *look,*'' she said. ''I'll want to see you ridin' around hereabouts, checkin','' she said.

She nodded again.

''Okay, you got a deal. Long as I see you ridin' about, *really, really* looking. I can make do with Bossy, Flower and Priscilla—but only until Susan Briggs's baby arrives.''

He knew that Susan Briggs had two previous children who had had to depend on Mrs. Nedlinger's goats for milk. There was no putting it off now, he'd *have* to go up and check on Alister as part of his investigation now that both goats and chickens were missing. He could put if off no longer.

First, he'd quietly check all the places close to town. Especially the ones that were a little isolated. See if anyone had ''new goats.'' Or a lot more chickens than they used to.

But in the meantime, something else—an even more immediate emergency—arrived as he left Mrs. Nedlinger's house and rode back to his office.

Chapter Five

"Some dang fool just robbed me," Ferd Cody yelled as Dan rode Sarah up the street. He came running from his general store toward Dan, huffing and puffing.

"He took off heading into the mountains," Ferd continued, trying to breathe hard and talk at the same time.

He bent over and balanced his elbows straight out with his hands propped on his thighs, to help himself breathe easier as he spoke.

"Which way did he go?"

"Jay Garrity said he passed him headin' up to the mountain to the left of Grizzly Butte."

One of the high mountains.

"What does he look like?" Dan said.

"Red hair, red mustache, red shirt, black trousers. City feller—leather shoes. You can't miss him. And if that's not enough, he has the biggest nose this side of the Mississipp','' Ferd said. ''No wonder he robs fer a livin',' ' he said, shaking his head in wonderment, regret, and maybe a little sorrow.

''If I weren't so dang mad, and need the money . . .''

''Ferd, you don't need to be sorry, or kindhearted, about a robber,'' Dan said.

Together, they went quickly into the office, and Dan picked up his rifle and some ammunition. His gun belt was already in place around his waist, something he did as soon as he put his trousers on in the morning.

After he relocked the door, Dan climbed into Sarah's saddle.

He could see that Ferd was worried; he was following close behind.

''Sarah and me've just been achin' for a ride up there into those mountains,'' he said to Ferd.

''If you're not back by dusk, I'll have Jay Garrity take care of yer livestock,'' Ferd said.

''Thanks,'' Dan said.

Stopping again quickly at his house to pick up a few food supplies, a bedroll and a canteen, he started off, carefully following the track that Jay Garrity had been only too happy to run out of the livery stable across the street from his office and show him as he rode by. The trail went east.

The man had probably forty-five minutes' head start.

Sure enough, the robber was heading up the mountain to the left of Grizzly Butte.

Dan followed the tracks, and at the end of the road to the east of town, they led upward following an old, faint trail that Dan was familiar with. From the left of Grizzly Butte, the tracks turned up onto Grizzly Butte itself. Grizzly

Butte was steep and the ascent rapid. Higher, in fact, than the mountain to the left that the man had started for.

By late afternoon, he could sense that the man was slowing, and he knew that it would not be long before he caught up to him.

A rueful look flitted across Dan's face as he realized what the man was going through.

In his getaway plans, going up into the mountains, the man had not counted on one thing: mountain sickness.

By ascending so fast, this obviously sea-level resident was getting sick.

And he'd done it to himself.

If he had remained calm, he'd have been all right, but apparently the excitement of the robbery and this fatiguing getaway were bringing on mountain sickness symptoms: headache, nausea, vomiting. There was ample evidence of this last item on the trail—dizziness, weakness, and well, loose bowels.

Dan came upon a very large area of talus—a pile of granite boulders which had fallen off higher up the mountain—blocking the robber's way.

The robber, knowing that the sheriff was close behind, had abandoned his tired horse. It was a horse that had seen better days and one that the people in town who knew horses would jokingly have called a "ten-dollar mustang"—an unflattering description.

The man had abandoned the ten-dollar mustang and begun trying to scramble across the talus.

Another mistake.

Not a mountain man, that was certain.

He was ahead of Dan, going up and down among the

boulders like a prairie dog lookout bobbing in his prairie-dog hole. Climbing up boulders and then climbing down.

A time-consuming process.

A novice on the mountain.

A flatlander.

Dan swung down off Sarah and took the time to carefully picket her.

He even took time to quickly picket the robber's horse.

To lose her up here would not be good for either of them. He had no desire to walk home to River Grove again, if, for some reason (like either being wounded or dead), the man ended up needing to be on the only horse available.

Then he began going over the talus the way that it should be done: instead of going up and down in between boulders, he stayed on the top of the pile of boulders.

To go up and down each time meant that you had to cover twice as much territory, as well as being tiring.

Dan moved smoothly and steadily, stepping from rock to rock, judging the stability of each rock as he carefully stepped on it.

If a rock tipped, he was always ready to hop to the next rock by carefully keeping his balance.

Something about the way Ferd had described his encounter with the robber led Dan to believe that he was dealing with a nonviolent man, but Dan was not about to gamble on it.

And secretly he was chuckling at the odd way the fleeing man was scrambling over the rocks. The need of the man for an outhouse—right now—was obvious to Dan.

He called out to the man in his most commanding voice, "This is the Sheriff! I'm not foolin' around with you. Put your hands up, *now!*"

Slightly to his amazement, the man did. He dropped the cloth bag that he was carrying on the nearest large boulder, and turned slowly around to face Dan.

He didn't appear to have a gun, or if he did it was in the cloth sack.

"Don't shoot, don't shoot!" the man said. "I'm geefing up."

Geefing must mean giving, Dan thought.

The man put his hands in the air.

"My mudder is goink to kill me," he said to Dan, "when she finds out what I done!"

Reaching him, Dan picked up the cloth bag the man had dropped, and they went back across the talus. Twice the man slipped and fell.

On the way back, Dan had to let the man rest, and stop for nature's call—it seemed to Dan like every few minutes.

They camped as dusk came. After Dan fed the man, they lay down—the robber to sleep, and Dan to lie awake. He gave the man Sarah's saddle blanket to roll up in.

Dan heard the man crying in the dark, as the coals from the fire grew low, just before he added some more brush to the fire.

Back in town the next day, Dan locked the man up in his office in the cell to the left. Jay Garrity and Ferd Cody came to stare at the man, proud of their part in his capture.

The prisoner sorrowfully emptied out his pockets and returned to Ferd the twenty-three dollars and forty-seven cents he had stolen. He handed it without comment to Ferd, through the bars of the cell. Ferd accepted the money, nodding to Dan as he took it that that was all of it.

Ferd was right about the man's nose. It was the largest nose Dan had ever seen on a man—or a woman.

''You're not cut out for a life of crime,'' Dan told the ruddy-faced man, who turned out to be meek-mannered. His name was Niles Olaf Turgstrom.

''You tink not?'' Niles said.

''I think not,'' Dan said. ''You better rest. It's the only cure there is for mountain sickness.''

Niles laid down on the cot with his face to the back wall as if he were ashamed, and sighed, the pockets of his pants still pulled inside out.

Chapter Six

Over the next week, Dan went on a quiet, methodical search for the goats, circling all through the River Grove area on Sarah.

First, he looked at the people who—in cowboy terms—"swung a wide loop," which meant that they were not averse to roping and stealing another man's cattle or livestock. Second, he looked at all the families that had some kind of a troublemaker in them. Third, he checked out people he thought might have a petty grudge against Mrs. Nedlinger.

That was quite a few people, once he thought about it.

He did all that without mentioning that any goats were missing.

But nothing.

Everybody seemed to be going about their business as

usual—however they did it, without the benefit of extra goats.

And not everyone was fond of goats.

After a few days, and every hunch played, he came up with nothing.

No sign of goats.

No goats anywhere.

No smell of goats, although these three missing goats were females, not males—which tended to smell a little stronger than females, he'd heard.

Nothing that looked or smelled like goat manure, either.

At church on Sunday, sitting two rows in front of Cassie Chadwick, Julia Anderson and Moira, he saw, somewhat with alarm, that Mrs. Brigg's belly looked a lot larger than it had last week.

She must be getting close.

Mrs. Nedlinger gave him what she considered a "secret look" from across the aisle. She looked at him with a frown and then directed his eyes with hers toward Mrs. Briggs's swollen belly. Mrs. Briggs was what his mother would have called "heavy with child." Her two children stood beside her, a boy and a girl.

He nodded a slight nod so that Mrs. Nedlinger would know that he understood.

Hurry up. Mrs. Nedlinger seemed to be saying.

Outside, after the service, Julia Anderson came up to him where he was standing off to the side, underneath an oak tree.

"What was that between you and Mrs. Nedlinger?" she asked.

He was flattered that she had been watching him.

"Business," he said, smiling.

He looked at her.

There had been some changes since Moira and Cassie's arrival.

Julia Anderson saw him looking at her new, probably freshly sewn dark green dress, and looked down and blushed.

"It was time," she said.

"I can't disagree with that," he said.

Now that he looked more carefully, he could see that her hair was no longer in a severe bun and, although still parted neatly in the middle, it was more softly waved to each side before continuing on into the bun at the back of her head.

It was a good improvement.

"How are you making out without your mother?" she said.

"Good, I guess." he said.

That was a lie. It was lonely all alone in the house in the meadow without someone to talk to. But why burden Julia Anderson with his troubles?

"Is Mrs. Chadwick all right staying with you a few days more?" he asked.

Julia smiled a warm smile and nodded. Evidently she and Cassie and Moira got along just fine.

"I enjoy having them," she said. "They are welcome to stay as long as they like."

Cassie and Moira walked out of the church, down the step, and came over to where he and Julia were standing under the oak tree to the right of the door of the church.

"I was just talking to the pastor," Cassie said, with a smile. "He seems very nice."

"We were just talking about you," Julia said to Cassie

with a smile. "I was just telling him that you and Moira are welcome to stay as long as you like."

Cassie's eyes glowed with happiness.

"We," she said, looking down at Moira and then glancing back up, "we love living in town. It's exciting! So many people. We were so lonely out at . . ." her voice trailed off rather than say Rattlesnake Gulch.

Dan smiled and said, "I can't agree more. Not a great place."

Julia said, "I can't believe how brave you were, to go and rescue Mrs. Chadwick and Moira like that. She told me all about it."

He didn't answer.

What could he say? That it was his fault that he didn't get out there sooner?

Cassie looked up at him, and then looked at Julia and added with intently raised eyebrows: "I felt very safe and protected with him." She was saying it to Julia, not to him, so he didn't have to respond. He was glad of that.

After saying their good-byes, Julia and Mrs. Chadwick and Moira left to go back home, and he strolled back up the street to his office, even though it was Sunday morning.

As he reached the built-up part of town, he came to the area of wooden sidewalks that connected most of the buildings and front porches. They were necessary because of the mud. He walked on the wooden sidewalk until he reached his own office.

Crooked Charlie was leaning up against the post holding up the left corner of the porch in front of his office, waiting for him.

Crooked Charlie, of all people, had a suggestion about what to do with Mrs. Chadwick. Crooked Charlie, an extraordinarily large man with long, shiny, full black hair parted in the middle and a huge black mustache, who owned the saloon named the Sharpsburg—a name that in itself often started trouble, what with so many Civil War veterans of both sides floating around.

And a man about whom it was prudent to find out the truth about his nickname *before* playing cards with him—although he had never been *caught* cheating. He'd come up with the idea.

And the idea was a good one, making Dan realize that it was no wonder Charlie had never been caught cheating—he was a smart son of a gun.

A man whose eyes always seemed sadly amused by some secret that he wasn't telling.

Crooked Charlie owned and had named the Sharpsburg Saloon, which was the next building on the right, next to Dan's office.

The name Sharpsburg was the Yankee name for a Civil War battle.

Rebels called that same battle the Battle of Antietam. Yankees named battles according to the nearest town; the Rebels named them according to the nearest body of water. The Battle of Antietam was the bloodiest day of the war. At Antietam Creek, near Sharpsburg, Maryland, the battle technically was a victory for the North, but in many ways a tragic turning point in the war because General George McClellan failed to follow Lee's retreating army across the Potomac River into Virginia. Many people felt that if he had, the war would have been over much sooner, maybe even years sooner, and a great many lives would have been spared.

But that was hindsight, as far as Dan was concerned. How could McClellan have known that, that day?

Still, it was an odd name for a Southerner's saloon in California; and one that had, in the past, caused trouble, especially after either a Rebel or a Yankee—or a bunch of either—had had a few too many whiskeys in the Sharpsburg.

As Dan unlocked the office and went inside, he was surprised to see Crooked Charlie follow him to the doorway. It was Dan who had gotten him to give up a practice he had of playing cards with a cocked pistol lying on the card table.

Like thousands of other men, Crooked Charlie had brought the same pistol that he had used in the war west with him. It was that pistol that he'd laid on the table, a "Confederate Colt." One of the most famous Confederate revolvers, it was a Griswold and Grier percussion revolver, made in Georgia. Its design closely copied the .36-caliber Colt Navy type so popular with the Northern soldiers. It had a smooth wooden handle grip and a round barrel. A good gun, Dan had to admit.

Crooked Charlie lounged against the door frame politely until Dan motioned him to come in and sit down.

Uneasily, Crooked Charlie took the same seat that Mrs. Nedlinger had chosen the day she came in, only he sat slouched down in the chair as if embarrassed to be caught talking to the sheriff, which Dan guessed he was.

They only had an uneasy truce; and only until and if Crooked Charlie was caught cheating. They both knew that.

"I want to discuss an idea I had with you," Charlie said. "I got an idea in mind for what I call the Two School Theory."

He paused.

Dan kept his face straight, trying not to indicate in any way how surprised he was that Crooked Charlie was discussing the educational needs of the community.

''Go on,'' Dan said.

In his polite Virginia gentleman's pleasant, soft voice with his Southern accent, Charlie continued. ''Children from a large area on both sides of town attend the one-room school out past Julia Anderson's house.''

Dan nodded, yes, he knew that. What was considered River Grove did cover a large area of land now.

The school was located just over a very low saddle-back—a low place between two ridges—outside of town. It was a five-minute walk west from town.

Horace Blackthorn was the very unpopular schoolteacher there. He was an old-fashioned spare-the-rod-and-spoil-the-child kind of man, and many of the smaller children were terrified of him and afraid to go to school, to the point of having ''bellyaches'' in the morning before school. He was about forty years old, short and thin, and had salt-and-pepper hair. He always wore a black frock coat.

In the past, rotten eggs—a real bad smell—had been thrown at the house where he boarded with the large Zachary family during the school year, but only on the side of the house where Horace's room was.

It had turned out to be some boys around eleven, twelve, and thirteen who attended Horace's school.

To Dan's mind it was the sign of a bad teacher when students went that far in retaliation. A person who was too strict and not fair caused that kind of hateful behavior.

When it turned out to be those particular boys, their parents had had to punish them.

But Dan personally wasted no respect or affection on Horace Blackthorn. Personally he felt that a teacher should be firm, but also good and kind, qualities he felt were greatly lacking in unmerciful Horace, who seemed to take a perverse delight in humiliating children.

But he wasn't the one who had chosen Horace. Horace was here long before Dan returned home and took over as sheriff.

"Horace's school is beginning to be overcrowded, what with all the new settlers," Crooked Charlie said tactfully, leaning back even further in the chair.

"A new school should be opened on the other side of town," he continued.

His suggestion made a lot of sense. Parents would be particularly happy that their children from Dan's own side of town would no longer have to walk past the four saloons to get to school.

"I heard that Mrs. Chadwick, that new widow lady, can read and write pretty good," Crooked Charlie said. "She could open a school in one of the abandoned buildings."

He was referring to the fact that quite a few abandoned buildings and shacks were still left both in town and outside of it after the height of the mining rush; when things died down after the mid-1850s. As the Gold Rushers left, they began to abandon the places where they had lived; sometimes even leaving just ghost towns in the mining areas, although there was still mining going on in some places.

Now newcomers wanted farmland and land for cattle ranching.

"A fairly decent square building sits just outside of

town, not that far from your place, in fact. The old Morris place. It needs only the dust and cobwebs swept away and minor alterations, and the school would just need someone to supply wood for the woodstove on a reg'lar basis to be up and running,'' Crooked Charlie added in his soft drawl.

Dan had to admit it was an idea worth thinking about.

Right after Charlie left, he walked back to the church and talked to Pastor Cook. The pastor was closing up the church and locking the door as he arrived.

''My, my,'' was all Pastor Cook said, when Dan told him whose idea it was, but he did mildly raise his pure white eyebrows in surprise so that they appeared over the tops of his eyeglasses.

''I think I can help you put this plan in motion,'' the pastor said. ''I can check with Mrs. Chadwick and do the rest of the planning.''

''Thank you, Pastor,'' Dan said, relieved. ''I have to go out of town for a few days. That would be a big help.''

''Glad to be able to be of service. Tell you the truth, I'm not all that happy with Horace's teaching. I'd like to have at least some of the students have an alternative.''

Dan nodded agreement, politely touched his hand to his hat, and left.

By late afternoon, the pastor walked over to the office to tell Dan what was arranged to happen while Dan was gone: Cassie Chadwick was to begin to teach nine students in the little Morris house between Mrs. Nedlinger's house and town, just down the road from Dan's property. Church members were to help clean the house and even supply the small amount of money for paper, chalk, books, and small slates to write on with the chalk. Ferd Cody was going to

give them a break on prices of school supplies; he was even donating some.

The small amount paid by the families to Cassie would enable her to begin to pay Julia Anderson for room and board. This arrangement would be fine with Julia. She would watch Moira. Cassie herself was very happy, also, relieved that she would have some way to make a living for herself and for her child, the pastor said.

The pastor had sure been busy.

As for himself, he could put if off no longer. He had exhausted all other possibilities, as far as he could see. He'd have to speak to Jay Garrity about taking care of Niles Olaf Turgstrom, the robber, who was still in jail, and taking care of Dan's livestock and chickens again.

Jay was Jeff Graywood's part-time helper at the livery stable, and Dan's part-time helper at the jail and at his home.

He could be counted on to take good care of Niles while Dan was gone. As for Dan, he'd have to go "up mountain" tomorrow and see if it *was* Alister Skinner who was stealing chickens and goats.

Chapter Seven

Heading out of town at dawn the next morning, Dan guided Sarah through the foothills, leading her gradually, with the reins held loosely through his fingers, into the increasingly steep hills and ravines that led up the mountain toward where Alister lived, high up on Grizzly Butte.

He had supplies with him on a medium-to-old gray-brown pack mule he had rented last night at the livery stable, not knowing how long it would take to locate Alister. Jeffrey Graywood, the man who owned the livery stable, had assured him last night that the old mule could do the job.

In fact, since Jeff was a good friend, he had come out to the house and helped pack Dan's supplies on the mule for him before Dan left this morning. Large canvas sacks hung from both sides of the large mule's back.

Jeff always claimed that nobody could pack a mule as good as he, himself, could. He was probably right.

Sarah's saddlebags were also full of supplies.

Until midmorning, he and Sarah and the mule did fine. The mule followed nicely up the footpaths and horse trails that led up to the foothills that jutted up more and more like cones and then got steeper and steeper until Dan knew that he was actually off the gentler hills and slopes of the foothills and onto the mountain itself.

The scenery became more wild and beautiful than even the beauty down below.

Rugged gorges, and crags jutting up high, and pines softly murmuring contrasted with the clear bubbling water cascading down steep slopes, in some places over sharp rocks.

Often he came upon oak and pine groves on the more level areas of the trail, and once on a ridge near some spruce he stopped to look down in a ravine at what used to be a gold-mining camp.

In his mind he could still picture men working down there on and around the riverbanks, either digging in the stream or searching the rocks higher up for gold stuck between upturned rocks that faced at a different angle than the current. Rocks that faced the same way as the current, he knew, would not act as a pocket to catch gold.

He looked down there for a minute before urging Sarah on with his knees. In his mind he could almost still hear the sounds of crowbar and pick, and men talking to each other down in the ravine. But it was probably only the breeze in the pines.

Old-timers had once told him that while they were mining, the noise they made often disturbed nearby wolves, and that the wolves would actually bark—not howl—at the miners in annoyance.

The rocky elevation began to make for rough traveling and at midmorning he felt the mule begin to tug backward on the lead he was holding, and to balk.

He realized that Sarah, also, was getting tired. Her sides were heaving, as they often did after a steep climb.

It was time to be kind.

''All right, all right, I know you're tired,'' he said, mainly to Sarah and only partly to the mule, and he got down.

He went back to check the mule. Although Jeff Graywood did a good job with packing this mule, it was time to check if the load had shifted, or if anything had gotten unbalanced. They had come a long way over rough territory.

The mule obviously thought it had. And a mule always values his own opinion.

All saddling and packing was done from the left side of a mule or burro, so as usual, Dan approached this mule on the mule's left side, being watchful of the mule's ears. He was well aware that a mule will not be aggressive without turning his ears back along his neck, a lot further back than when he is just listening to something behind him.

This mule's ears were normal.

He thought over whether to go to the trouble of totally unloading the mule's load to check for something bothering his back, like a pebble. Then he thought, no. Better to just check first to see if anything was just off balance.

He had to give Jeff some credit for brains.

He figured that Jeff knew enough after all these years to

thoroughly groom the mule's back to remove dirt, salt, and sand before putting the blanket on, and to put the blanket too far forward and then slide it back so that the mule's hair will lie smooth, as his own father had taught him.

If he had to take a guess, he would guess that he was not as good a mule packer as Jeff Graywood. If he did unpack the mule and then repack, it would take probably twenty minutes to half an hour, and he might end up replacing the supplies unbalanced.

Leave well enough alone, and just check to see if anything has shifted.

Yes, it had. One of the mule's large canvas bags had drifted into a crooked position. He readjusted it.

The mule seemed satisfied.

If it was a burro he was with, he would have to be careful to make friends with the burro. A burro detects friendship very quickly. But a mule doesn't care so much if you like him or not.

This particular mule looked as if he couldn't care less.

Burros liked the bunch grass that grew here, on this higher ground. This mule looked like he was waiting for Dan to give him oats.

His father used to joke that a mule was one end that kicks, another end that bites, and a stubborn jackass in the middle. But even he had had to admit that a mule was not stupid.

Dan made up his mind to stop at the next stream and let his horse and the mule drink and rest.

It was only fifteen minutes later that he came to the stream that he had in mind. It was a stream that contained what the locals called cobble, fairly large rounded rocks in the water that reminded people of cobblestones.

He slowly and carefully walked both animals across, and let them rest on the other side, as well as drink.

The rest of the day went well. The mule didn't balk again. By early evening, he decided to make camp. As a sheriff, usually when he was camping he circled back around the trail to make camp where he could see if anyone was on his trail, but this time he felt it was not necessary.

He pulled off the trail to a level place where there was grass enough for Sarah and the mule, and took off Sarah's saddle and unpacked the mule. He let the animals drink from a nearby stream before picketing them and feeding them each a few handfuls of oats from the mule's pack.

The mule seemed to like that.

Dead branches were off to the side here, and stumps of great downed trees and tree limbs were strewn about. It was an area of pines and rocky crags and quartz outcroppings.

Then he made his own supper. He heated up some buck stew he'd brought in a tin container and ate it with some coffee and biscuits.

Then he spread out his bedroll.

He slept with his pants legs carefully tucked into his socks, so that critters didn't crawl in during the night.

The next morning, after they again had all eaten and drunk, he checked the mule's back for any sores. It was fine, so he packed the mule back up, and they were on their way shortly after dawn. He wasn't sure if he would reach Alister Skinner's cabin today or tomorrow.

The day passed uneventfully, as they wound on upward. It was shortly after four o'clock when he came to a cabin in a clearing and he yelled, ''Hallo, the house,'' as was proper to do before approaching anyone's cabin.

At first, there was no answer.

He picketed Sarah and the mule in the trees out of sight of the cabin.

He called again.

This time, he thought he heard a very muffled noise coming from inside the cabin.

Chapter Eight

Loosening his gun from his holster so that it would pull out easily, he cautiously approached the cabin door. With his right hand—he was a left-handed shooter—he knocked on the door.

He thought he heard a muffled sound; he thought someone was saying "Come in," but he wasn't sure.

If he stood in the doorway, his back to the light, he would make a fine profile of a target as he opened the door for the person inside. And as his eyes adjusted to the darkness inside, the inside person would still have all the advantage. So, standing to the right of the door, he threw open the door wide—it opened inward creaking loudly—and stepped back out of the way. There was no telling what kind of a reception the old codger inside was about to give him. A shotgun blast—both barrels—was not entirely out of the question, especially if Alister Skinner had been

sneaking around town stealing goats and chickens and knew the law was after him.

Instead, there was silence.

''Hello,'' Dan said.

''Help,'' a deep, but very weak-sounding voice inside the cabin said.

Was it a trick?

Dan let his gut feeling decide for him.

His gut feeling was that it was a genuine cry for help.

He entered the cabin.

It looked and smelled like a place that indeed had been housing a sick person for a period of time. Food was spoiling on plates as if a person who was too weak to wash dishes lived there. Indeed, dirty dishes were strewn about, near the bed, on the floor, and on a hand-hewn table next to the bed frame made of pine logs. All the wooden water buckets were empty and dried out, like they hadn't held water in a long time. On the bed lay a man who Dan imagined was Alister Skinner, a man Dan had only heard about. He looked like he was over fifty years old.

He was dressed in a blue and white plaid shirt that had seen better days; it was faded and tattered, but reasonably clean. His trousers were wrinkled and dirty, and he had a long gray beard. He was very thin, which made his somewhat pointy nose appear even narrower, and below that the gray beard was growing out of control in a scraggly manner.

The skin on his hands and face, however, as sick as he appeared to be, were clean. So was the cabin, which Dan saw as he quickly glanced around looking for another person. There was no one else in the room except the old man.

"Help," he called out again. When he saw Dan enter, he spoke.

Not to Dan, but looking up to the ceiling, with his hands folded as if in prayer, he said, "Thank you, God."

Then he looked back over at Dan.

"My leg," he said, in explanation.

Dan went over to the bed, which was a bunklike thing in the far back left-hand corner of the cabin and looked. One trouser leg was cut open to above the knee.

Alister Skinner was not the chicken or goat thief. His left leg looked like it had been injured for some time. The deep wound was just below his knee on his left leg, on the outside part, but on the kneecap itself just enough to make the knee stiff when it healed.

"Two weeks ago, I cut my knee accidentally with my axe," the man said. "Festered up pretty bad, there, ain't it?"

Dan nodded.

Alister Skinner was darn lucky that he didn't have lockjaw with a wound as bad as this one.

Dan gently covered the wound up with a blanket for the time being. He had work to do.

"Let me see what I can do," Dan said.

Alister seemed to have fallen back asleep, or passed out, Dan didn't know which. He felt the man's head, no fever. That was good. It probably meant that the man would be all right, if Dan could do something about the terribly infected knee.

It didn't look like gangrene. That was a good sign also.

Dan took two buckets and went outside to locate the stream. It was directly in back of the cabin, down a fairly steep grassy slope. No wonder the injured man couldn't get water with that knee. If he'd gone down the slope, he would not have been able to get back up.

He filled the two buckets from the clear, cold, fast-running stream and brought them back to the house. Alister had only a fireplace, not a woodstove. Dan went back outside to gather wood. When he had an armload of various sizes, he went back inside.

Starting the fire in the fireplace, he swung the black wrought-iron teakettle out from the fire and filled it with water, and then swung the wrought-iron rod with the teakettle hanging from it back into the fire to heat.

He looked around and found some soap, some salt, and some flour, and not much else.

He went out to Sarah and got the sack hanging from his saddle. It had coffee and deer jerky, biscuits, and even some of last night's leftover potatoes in it.

While the man slept and the water heated, Dan went back out and brought Sarah and the mule closer to the house, and watered and then picketed them.

He unsaddled Sarah and unpacked the mule, this time carrying everything off the mule into the cabin.

Inside the door, he dumped everything on the floor.

He had to get the disgusting yellow stuff out of the wound. That was his first job.

But how?

He had none of his mother's remedies available. The only two things he saw in the cabin or in his things that might be useful was the salt and the soap.

Both would sting like a son of a gun.

But what choice did he have, if he wanted to save the old man's life—or leg?

Some people would have poured whiskey on the wound.

He didn't have any of that, and if the man had had any he would have used it by now. He looked around the cabin anyway. There was none that he could find.

The water was getting warm enough to use. What to use? The salt or the soap?

Both.

Dan found a piece of linen and cut it into a large square. Then he washed it in warm soapy water, rinsed it in another bowl of water, and then wrung it out. He washed out a battered-looking blue enamel basin and dumped all the used soapy water outside the cabin door. Then he refilled the clean basin with more warm soapy water, and throwing back the gray woolen blanket, he began to wash out the cut, pulling out the yellow matter that was in the wound.

Alister stirred and moaned, and cried out a few times. Then he awakened and looked down at what he seemed to agree needed to be done. He sank back on the bed, grimacing but silent.

Dan was impressed with his courage.

Dan washed and washed until the wound was clean, turning and folding the cloth to clean areas as he worked.

It was not a pleasant job.

When he was done, there was a deep V in the man's leg, but it was clean.

Not knowing what to do next, he decided to make a weak solution of saltwater and try that. He washed another small bowl and put about a teaspoon of salt in it, and then added hot water from the kettle.

He put it aside to cool.

He heated up the food he'd brought inside and fed Alister and himself.

Now, much as he hated to, he'd have to do laundry.

There was no sense putting dirty clothing or blankets on that wound.

He went outside to start a fire in front of the cabin. It was getting dark, but by firelight, he managed to wash some of the older man's clothing and a blanket he'd found in the corner of the cabin and hung them on bushes and shrubs to dry. They'd not start to dry until the sun came out in the morning, but at least they would be clean.

Inside, he lit an oil lamp.

The saltwater had cooled, so he folded another section of wet linen he had washed into a small padlike square and dipped it into the saltwater and patted it on the wound for fifteen minutes at a time, every hour all through the night.

Chapter Nine

He wasn't altogether sure, but by morning, he thought that the area surrounding the wound looked a little less red and angry looking.

He went outside after dawn and fed Sarah and the mule some more oats, watered them, and then went back in and fell asleep on the floor of the cabin.

It was early afternoon when he woke up. His mouth felt dry and terrible. The fire had burned down to coals on the verge of going out. He added more wood to the fire to get it going again.

Alister was still sleeping so Dan went outside with the two buckets and made still another trip down the slope to get water. Even if the older man's leg healed without his knee being permanently stiff, Dan doubted if he could get down to this water from his cabin. He'd have to talk to

Alister Skinner about taking him back to town, at least until they could see if and how well his leg healed.

When the man woke up, Dan asked him, "How are you feeling, Mr. Skinner?"

"Call me Alister," the man said, grinning. "Makes me feel old when you call me Mr. Skinner. I'm just a young whippersnapper."

Dan chuckled. The older man still had a sense of humor.

For two more days Dan went through the ritual of cleaning and then using the saltwater compresses on the man's pale white knee. The older man's skin was paper thin, and the bluish veins showed through.

Once, Dan joked, "This is *not* a leg of great beauty," as he gently worked on it. The older man chuckled, as if he agreed.

It seemed to be getting better, but it was going to be a long time before the man could fend for himself.

The same thought had at least passed through Alister's mind, Dan realized on the third day as Alister stirred, and then woke up, late in the afternoon. He'd gone to sleep shortly after lunch. It wasn't so much what the man said, as how he looked regretfully around the cabin at his things—almost as if making a picture in his mind to remember.

Dan saw him looking at his sheriff's badge, not with the frightened look a man who had something to hide sometimes looked at it, but with the look that meant he realized that Dan was a man who had a job to do back in town and Alister knew that Dan couldn't stay away from it too long.

In fact, Alister had, when Dan stopped to think about it,

the look of a man—despite the leg situation—at peace with himself.

Not a crook.

And it was Alister who brought up the subject of town while Dan was busy making Alister and himself something to eat, using a very old black frying pan that was blackened on the outside by many fires over the years, probably both in this cabin and in campfires on many trails.

"Flapjacks, is that what you're makin' fer supper?" Alister inquired.

Dan shook his head, yes.

"Are you plannin' on haulin' me back to town?" Alister said next.

"Thinkin' on it," Dan admitted, taking a minute to glance over and look Alister in the eye to assess how Alister felt about it.

"Thought you might," Alister admitted.

"You got any objections to that?" Dan asked mildly.

"Can't see that if I did it'd make any difference," Alister said, in a resigned but not angry way. "Sized up the situation, and can't, myself, see no other possibility."

"I'm sorry."

"Don't be. Was bound to happen, sooner or later. Tell you the truth, always thought that when my time come, I'd just lie here and die, in the mountains."

He grinned, a weak grin.

"But when the time came to do that I jest didn't feel like dying, is all. Wanted to go on livin'. If you hadn't come along—well, I might have been a goner in a few more days. Seems like I was gettin' too durn weak to get up and go fetch water and feed myself."

He didn't mention running out of supplies, but they were both aware of it.

Dan's thoughts flew to the worry about how Alister could afford to live in town, if that was how he was planning to spend the rest of his days.

It seemed as if Alister read his mind—perhaps a look of worry had crossed his face—but the old man grinned.

"Jest before we was to get on your horse and go on down into town, I'd be much obliged if you'd pry up the third floorboard over there," he said, grinning and pointing at the floorboard in question.

"And I'm also mighty relieved that it was a sheriff what come to take me back to town."

He grinned again.

"I couldn't have asked for more. Kind of like my own personal bodyguard."

He pointed to a crowbar that sat perched on two big nails—spikes really—on the wall area that was behind the door when the door was swung open.

"Aw, go ahead, now," he said, happily. "I'd like to see it again, myself. Cheers me all up. Go ahead," he urged.

Smiling at the older man's barely covered-up glee, Dan took the old, beat-up crowbar off the two nails and went to where the old man indicated.

Sticking one end of the crowbar under the end of the plank, he pried it up. Nails squeaked as the crowbar forced them up out of the pine boards.

Underneath was a deep hole.

"Watch out fer spiders," Alister warned him chuckling. Dan didn't know if it was a joke or not, but he was careful as he stuck his hand down in the deep hole, pulling up one heavy bag after another until there were six large bags beside the hole in the floor.

Gold.

''So, you think that'll do me 'til I croak?'' Alister said.

''Yes, old man, I do,'' Dan said, in a teasing way. ''How come you trust me?''

''I'm old, but I'm not a fool. Don't make the mistake of thinking that just because someone is old, that their brains have shriveled up.''

Dan thought of his mother and father.

''I don't, old man.''

''No, you probably don't. Well, some do. Anyway, I been watchin' you care—kindly, I might add—for a man that as far as you could see don't have a pot fit to take a leak in.''

He was right. Dan had judged him to be destitute.

''Ask you one thing?'' Dan inquired.

''Ask away. Ask as many questions as you like. Saved my life; the way I figger it, I owe you.''

''I was wondering where you got your supplies. The closest town is Little Sa . . . River Grove, and I've never seen or heard of you going there.''

''That's because I ain't never come there. Wouldn't be goin' there now if it wasn't that you're from there and I ain't got no *choice.*''

His leg must have pained him, because he'd inadvertently moved it as he was speaking. He grimaced. Dan got up and helped him get comfortable again. He uncovered the wound to let the air get at it.

''Heard a while back that the snooty citizens down there changed it. Just as well. Don't want them using a good name if they don't appreciate it.''

He hadn't answered the question that Dan had asked, and he seemed to suddenly remember it.

"Oh, about supplies. Before I got hurt I used to go all the way to Red Bluff to get my supplies."

"All that way to avoid going to Little Sage?"

"Yep."

"Why?"

Dan knew that he had gone way over the boundary of what and how many questions it was polite and good manners to ask strangers. But by now, he was simply curious. Why go so far out of your way to avoid Little Sage?

Too late, he remembered Mrs. Nedlinger and her stories about Alister scalping his mistress.

Again, the older man seemed to read his mind.

Chapter Ten

"No," he said softly. "I never scalped my wife. Gossipers say she was my mistress, but that was not true any more than it was true that I scalped her. The truth was that we were married for twelve, maybe thirteen years and she got a turrible thing growing right on the top of her head."

He pointed to his own head to show an area right in the top middle part of his hair and he drew his hand back to right in the center of the crown of his head.

"The doc over in Red Bluff said it was 'a cancer.' I didn't know what the heck 'a cancer' even was. Never heard of it. Anyway, Edith and I tried everythin'. Every supposed 'cure' that anyone had, or told us about. We bought every elixir available. She took every teaspoon of every elixir we bought.

"It kept growing.

"The doc over in Red Bluff just shook his head. He

didn't know what to do any more than we did. The worse''—Dan knew he meant to say worst—''was that someone said that they had cured a cancer on someone up north by scraping off the bad stuff with a knife and then pouring gunpowder and prairie sorrel on it.

''So some friends of ours brought us some prairie sorrel and we mixed it with gunpowder and they helped us put it on the cancer so it would go away.''

His forehead creased with worry and sorrow as he spoke. ''Edith screamed like the dickens when we did it. I didn't *want* to. She *made* me. Made us *both* cry.''

He paused, unembarrassed to say he had cried. He was a tough man.

''*Don't ever, ever do that to anybody you love.* It was a plumb loco idea. The people who tole us to try it said it had dried up the cancer on the person up north and it fell off in a big scab in a few weeks. Didn't work for Edith. Think now it was just one of those crazy stories that somehow get tole.

''Word got around that I scalped her. Nothing was further from the truth. Broke my heart when she passed away. Cancer ate right through her. It was horrible beyond words. I seen men scalped and who lived who looked better than Edith did at the end. But I sure loved her. She was only thirty when she died.''

''So that was why you didn't want to go to Little Sage?''

Alister looked surprised.

''Why no,'' Alister said, raising his eyebrows in surprise. ''It was because of bankers. I hate bankers: idiots, crooks and scoundrels, that's what they are. All idiots, crooks, or dirty scoundrels! Especially Harvey King. Him I hate the worst. That's why I don't go to Little Sage or River Grove or whatever fancy name it's called these days,'' he said sarcastically.

Then he added with great feeling, ''It's because of that crook, Harvey King. It's *loyalty* to Edith that made me go somewheres else all these years. That crook, King, stole all Edith's money before I married her.

''Edith was orphaned in a cholera epidemic when she was seventeen. After the funeral, when she went to the bank, Harvey tole her that she didn't have no money in there. She knew for a fact that there was eight thousand dollars in Harvey King's bank in her and her parents' name. Harvey just kept that money for himself. Luckfully,''—Dan knew he meant luckily—''Edith married me and we went off before I blew Harvey's brains from here to Kingdom Come.

''Me dirt poor and him rich, I'd have had a California collar for sure.''

A California collar was the name for the rope around your neck when you were hung from a tree.

''She made me leave town. Said nobody would believe her. Said it was her word against Harvey King: banker, prominent churchgoer, and family man. She was probably right.

''If I brought money into Little Sage, I figgered it would end up in the bank in the hands of Harvey King.''

He scratched his bearded chin.

''That's why I got to figger out a way to do something with that,'' he pointed at the gold bags, ''so that Harvey King don't get none of it. The man has mold in his hay.''

He meant that something about him was no good, rotten.

There was something that rang true about Alister's story.

The story put Dan in mind of the Barry boy. What was

his name, he thought, Dennis? Maggie and Enright Barry had died this past winter and Dan remembered being slightly surprised when the boy had had to go and live with a kindly family who had lost their own two children a while back.

He had been surprised to hear that the Barry boy had nothing; it had appeared that the family was fairly well-to-do. King had told everybody that when the family's debts were paid, there was nothing left. There was no reason to question it at the time. Now Dan began to wonder.

And five years ago the same thing had happened to K. G. James. Only he'd just heard about it through gossip when he got home. He was wearing the blue uniform of the U.S. Army when that happened, and a long way from home.

"If you don't mind, Alister, I think tomorrow we'll see if we can start to get you down the mountain."

"What about the gold?"

"Well, we can stash what supplies we don't need for the trip down here in your cabin. Just take what we need with us. Two bags of gold on the horse and four on the mule ought to do just fine. We'll divide it up. Especially as we'll be taking it easy."

He indicated Alister's still stiff, straight-out knee.

The big mule could carry up to four hundred pounds, maybe even more Dan figured.

The next morning just after dawn, Alister waited while Dan, out of respect for the older man, cleaned the cabin and left it orderly in case he was able to return. The extra food supplies were stored up high on shelves.

When they started out, they would be going slowly to see how Alister made out. The knee had to be bent a little to ride, and Dan was sure that Alister was already in pain just leaving the cabin, leaning on Dan for support. He hoped that the knee wouldn't split open and begin to bleed as they rode.

Dan helped Alister get up on Sarah. He would be riding behind Alister, bareback, on the mule. The empty canvas supply sacks were now filled with the gold. So were Sarah's saddlebags, which had the two smallest bags of gold in them.

He watched to see if Alister was all right, as they rode out of the clearing and went into the pines, back onto the trail that he had followed up to Alister's cabin. Now they'd be backtracking down that same trail to River Grove.

A few minutes into the ride back down the mountain, as Alister and Dan were just about to navigate downward in a particularly steep area, Alister looked down at Sarah as she picked her way carefully down the slope, and spoke regretfully: "Me, whose ole time cowboy philosophy was 'Take care of yer own darn self'—me, Alister Skinner, laid up, almost dyin' and gettin' help from a sheriff, no less. Boy has times changed. My pride is a little hurt."

"Everyone needs help from time to time, old man. I wouldn't worry about it." Dan said.

"Still, I wouldn't want my ole cowboy pals from down Texas way to know about this."

Dan grinned. The mule was picking its way down the same slope now, following at a safe distance behind Sarah.

"Your secrets are safe with me."

Dan meant the gold as well as what Alister was worrying about. Then he thought his promise over, and added one thing.

"All but the 'scalping your mistress' part. I want to correct a few people's version of the story on that."

The thought occurred to him how friendly Mrs. Nedlinger was with Harvey King, and how the whole story might have begun to get so widely circulated in the first place. Maybe Harvey King had used Mrs. Nedlinger to further spread the rumor about the "scalping."

Once, Alister pointed to a bed of scree—gravel—and said, "Cut off about twenty-five minutes if we cross near the edge of that, instead."

He meant instead of following the switchbacking trail around the scree the way Dan had come.

He looked back for Dan's okay, and after receiving it, Alister began easing Sarah onto a way he obviously knew around the bed of scree.

Sure enough, Dan was pleasantly surprised to see that Alister's way had cut off a nice chunk of circular trail. They came out near the ravine that Dan had stopped to look into on his way up.

Dan was impressed.

It had saved some time.

Time.

He hoped Mrs. Briggs hadn't had the child yet.

"What do you think about the transcontinental railroad going through down south, through Sacramento and all?" Alister asked. "Might bring some more changes. More people. Even more settlers to this area."

"Maybe, maybe not. Some don't care for the ruggedness or isolation of these kinds of mountains and foothills. Most will probably settle in the Sacramento Valley. More fertile. Fruit trees, and more wineries and the like. People call it an Eden."

"Mebbee so." Alister agreed. Then with a wicked grin

he said, "At any rate, the railroad will all but eliminate the need for the Donner party choice of food."

Dan said, "Alister, that's a terrible thing to say." He added jokingly, "You sure you weren't one of them scary Donner people?"

"Nah. Anyways, tole you that I come up from the south."

Dan knew that he meant the southwest.

"Anyways, it's already spoilt here. It ain't been the same here since '53," Alister continued regretfully, the fingers of one hand spread out over his upper leg now as he rode, holding the reins in his other hand.

Dan knew that he meant 1853—the height of the gold rush.

"By '55 or so, things had petered out here for the gold miner. Dang mining corporations taking over, tunneling deep into them hills. Some of my friends left for Nevada. Mining camps I knew was abandoned."

He was quiet for a few seconds and then Alister said in Spanish, "*Una gran sierra nevada.* Do you know what that means?"

Dan said, "Yes. A great snowy range."

"That's how this area got its name. Priest, I heard. From Mexico or Spain, I ferget which. He named it." Alister said.

"I only skirted the edges, you know." Alister continued, regretfully, looking back up at the mountain behind him. "Local Indians that I know, go in the highest areas of these mountains only on the best days of the summer."

Alister thought a minute, then added, "Smart."

A doe with two fawns bounded away as the two men came into a meadow clearing.

"You ever listen to yellow ponderosa pine? Makes more of a hum than other pines. But now you take yer lodgepole, it has more finely grained bark, if you look close."

Alister had had no one to talk to for so long, that he was wearing Dan out with talk. Dan had made a great effort to be polite, but he was hardly listening to the old man's chattering on about what he knew. He was worried about what to do with Alister when they got below.

They passed an outjutting of very pretty quartz. Some of it looked like marble, all milky, and other parts of it looked clear. It was on the back of an area of rock, so that Dan had missed seeing this particular outcropping on the upward trail. It looked interesting. . . .

When Dan didn't answer, Alister's talking trailed off into silence.

Dan almost laughed out loud when Alister said, out of the blue about a half an hour later: "When I get to town, I want to have a big breakfast. Bacon, sliced, pan-fried 'taters, biscuits, and *a great big pile of scrambled eggs.*"

Stolen chickens was one of the things that had brought Dan up here. And Alister was dreaming about eggs!

After this, Alister grew silent. He was all talked out and he was getting tired. Dan had to help him down from the horse.

They made camp silently, about an hour before dusk.

As they rolled up in blankets for the night, Alister asked Dan one more question.

"You ever hit pay dirt?"

"No, but I've cleaned out a few pockets in my time."

It made Dan wonder where it was that Alister had "hit pay dirt." He obviously had.

But it was a question that he couldn't ask.

The next morning, Sunday, Alister was again silent as they broke camp. The exertion of the previous day was showing. He looked pretty wrinkled and haggard.

Dan felt sorry for him.

"Not too much farther," he said.

After an hour of riding, Dan asked him if he wanted to stop and rest, but Alister shook his head no.

"Let's get this over with."

In the silence, Dan remembered something that he had long forgotten. Something that Alister's stories had brought to mind. There was a large wooden box of old records of mining claims full of erasures, changes and mutilations, along with a lot of other legal papers, stored, of all places, up in one of the lofts above the blacksmith's shop. The blacksmith had been, at one time, a judge here in town. The "judge" had long since retired, but his records were still stored up in the loft. Unless someone had thrown them out. They went back a lot of years, and had a lot of paperwork from the land office, unless he was mistaken.

Maybe he would go up there and drag the big wooden box out, and take a look through them. Maybe have a talk with the old judge.

"What did you say was your wife Edith's maiden name?" Dan asked when they stopped for lunch.

"I didn't," Alister Skinner said. "But her maiden name was Maxwell. Edith Raines Maxwell."

They crossed the stream where Dan had watered Sarah and the mule at midmorning the first day.

When they got close to town, a cow was standing in the road near Dan's own house. The cow was guarding her calf. It was not Dan's cow.

A man in Eastern clothes, a black woolen suit and a

black silk stovepipe hat came riding up the road. In a jubilant mood, probably from looking at the cow and her calf, he waved a big friendly wave at Dan and Alister.

Luckily, Sarah was well trained and the mule was used to fools. But it was the wrong thing to do: you *never* wave at a man on a horse. You might spook the horse. In fact it was an old Indian trick that Apaches of the Southwest used, to wave a red blanket or cloth at a horse so it might rear up and throw its rider. Especially as you rode into a battle. It was very effective.

Alister snorted in disgust at the Easterner's bad manners.

A nod is the proper greeting to a person on a horse. Or a polite "Howdy," Dan and Alister both knew. In fact, when coming up from behind, it was good manners to say a loud friendly greeting *before* you got within range of a pistol shot: "Hulloa, stranger."

The man passed by, and Dan couldn't resist turning his head just a bit as he rode along to see if the man looked back.

"Yep." Alister agreed, also peeking back at the rapidly retreating man. "Greenhorn."

After you passed, you didn't look back. It could insult someone with a quick temper or even worse, a quick trigger finger. It was an insult. To look back implied mistrust—that you thought the man would shoot you in the back, a dishonorable thing.

Dan made a mental note to talk to the stranger if he saw him again. The stranger better learn some things quick before his stay in California turned into something he hadn't planned on.

Chapter Eleven

Dan knew what he would be seeing and hearing about soon enough, people's shocked reaction to his bringing Alister to town: *The man who had scalped his wife was staying with the sheriff!* But he had made his decision.

He could just hear in his mind the buzzing of town gossip about it. People would be shocked and scared; at least until the truth got out about the cancer.

He didn't feel right about dumping Alister at the hotel in town with his leg still needing caring for, and with only gold as payment for his room and board. That would set a lot of tongues to wagging. Even worse, it could put Alister in danger. This way, even if word of the gold somehow leaked out, some might think twice about robbing someone staying with the sheriff in his own home.

Better to keep a low profile until Alister could figure out

what to do so that none of the money ended up at Harvey King's bank, as Alister had vowed.

It was lucky that Dan's house was on the outskirts of town so that no one except the Easterner and the mother cow had seen how heavy the horse and the mule's burden was.

The Easterner had shown no sign of comprehension at all, not even glancing once at the saddlebags and belongings of the two riders. Not even noticing the odd fact that the *sheriff* was on a mule, bareback.

As for the townspeople, as soon as the word spread, most probably would first think that Alister was going to be, or was, under arrest and going to jail as soon as his leg was good enough. They were in for a few surprises as far as the old man was concerned. Not the penniless old geezer they thought he was, for one thing.

When they reached Dan's house, Dan helped the old man down off the horse and into the house, and then he unloaded the mule in front of the door, close to the house.

Both the mule and Sarah were very tired. So was he.

Inside, he put Alister in his parent's bedroom, and helped Alister hide the gold under the bed. Alister armed himself just in case, leaving a pistol near his pillow. However, he looked out of place under Dan's mother's pink, green and white calico quilt.

Then Dan went back outside and took the mule to the barn, and gave him oats and water. He left the barn door open as it was a nice day. Tomorrow he'd return him to the livery stable. He fed and watered Sarah; her day was not through yet.

Leaving Alister comfortably set up in the bedroom, Dan

left for the office on Sarah. When he entered, Jay Garrity was removing a plate that Niles had finished with, through the hole for that purpose in the bars.

"Been a good prisoner," Jay said about Niles. "We been gettin' along just fine."

"Good." Dan said, shortly. "Anything else going on in town?"

"No," Jay said. "Been quiet."

"Mrs. Briggs's baby. Any news there?"

If Jay was surprised at the inquiry, he gave no sign. He put the empty plate and spoon on a corner of Dan's desk.

Niles still was sipping from a tin coffee cup.

"Not that I heard."

Dan felt that Jay was waiting for a bit of praise, so he looked around his office and nodded in satisfaction.

"Good job, Jay."

Jay looked pleased.

He picked up the plate and spoon. "Be back for the coffee cup later." Politely touching his fingers to his wide-brimmed, flat, black hat, the small wiry man left.

"Vats goink to hoppen to me?" Niles asked.

Dan was sure that Jay and he had discussed this while he was gone.

"It's not for me to say. Judge Herbert will hear your case and decide next week. I'm sorry. I wish I could tell you more."

"It's my tempers," Niles said, dejectedly. "Gets me into all da troubles."

"Will you be all right for a while if I go talk to someone for about a half hour?"

"Ya," Niles said. "Jay see you go, he'll come and check

on me, anyways. He gone come get da coffee cup back in few minutes. We friends, I tink."

"That's good," Dan said.

"You tink I get da noose around my neck, here?" Niles said.

"Sorry, I don't know. It's anybody's guess."

Niles nodded, ready to accept his fate.

"Where's your mother?" Dan asked.

"Back in olt country. Good ting. Wouldn't want her to see this." He indicated the cell, regretfully.

Outside the office, Dan got back up on Sarah and rode out toward his house, then turned left on the road branching off that led to Mrs. Nedlinger's house.

About two miles past Mrs. Nedlinger's house he pulled up in front of a cabin that belonged to the family that had taken Dennis Barry in when his parents had died this last winter.

Mrs. Richards and Dennis came out of the house.

"Well, hello, Sheriff. Heard your horse when you rode up."

She turned to Dennis and said, "Go fetch Mr. Richards. He's down by the barn."

The boy ran off toward the barn.

"Don't know what I'm going to do with that boy," Mrs. Richards said as soon as he left. "It's not working out. He runs off into the woods all the time; we never know where he is. Hardly ever goes to school when we think that that's where he is. It's just not the same as . . ." She left unsaid "as with our own children," but Dan knew that was what she was thinking.

Her own two children had died in an influenza epidemic two years ago. A boy and a girl. The boy was ten and the girl eight when they died. It was the same epidemic that had killed his own father.

"I'm sorry," Dan said. "What I wanted was to ask you about Maggie and Enright Barry, Dennis's parents."

Mrs. Richards seemed not alarmed, but surprised. Maybe a bit annoyed.

"Why ask about them? They've been dead quite a while. Can't see what good that will do." She looked over and seemed relieved that Dennis was running back so she didn't have to talk more.

Out of breath, Dennis ran up to them and said, "He'll be here in a minute. He's doing the four o'clock milking. We only got one milk cow."

Mrs. Richards said, "If you'll excuse me, I've got something on the stove." With a not-too-friendly look at Dennis standing there beside Dan, she left and went back inside, her black skirts swishing as she turned. She looked like a severe woman.

Dan swung down off Sarah, and walked her over into the shade of a giant oak tree about thirty feet from the house. Dennis followed.

They both stood there under the tree.

Dan and Dennis were both silent, waiting. A few minutes passed. There was no sign yet of Mr. Richards.

Finally, to break the silence, Dennis asked, "You ever find out who stole Mrs. Nedlinger's goats?"

Now it was Dan who was surprised. It took him a minute, but then he answered: "Yes. *I just did.* You see, no one but myself, Mrs. Nedlinger, and the *thief* knew that they were missing."

Dennis's eyes widened.

"It weren't my fault I took the goats; I *had* to. Mrs. Nedlinger didn't love them like I did."

He started to cry.

"Nobody loves them like I do. They love me back, too. And I take good care of them, even if does get me in trouble here," he said, looking rather sadly through his still dripping tears toward the door that Mrs. Richards had entered.

Dan tried not to let on how surprised he was at this turn of events. It took him a few seconds to collect his thoughts.

"Where are they?" Dan asked glancing around. "Are they here?"

"I got them in a pen up in the hills over there," Dennis said, pointing off in the distance, looking as if he were amazed at the stupidity of Dan to even think that they might be here on the Richards's property.

Then he added, still crying, "Are you going to whup me?"

"No. Does anyone here 'whup' you?"

"Sometimes. When I am bad."

"Do you like it here?"

"No. Mrs. Richards doesn't like me."

"I guessed as much."

"She says I ain't as good as her own children."

Dan didn't answer.

There was still no sign of Mr. Richards.

"Do you like Mr. Richards?"

"He's all right," Dennis said, a little reluctantly.

"Did Mr. Richards say he was coming?"

"Yes. But maybe he's having trouble in the barn."

"Maybe we'll take a walk over there," Dan said, beginning to lead Sarah over toward the barn.

Just then Mr. Richards came out. He was a sad, tired, defeated-looking man.

Dan decided that the goat thing was enough for today. The other questions—what he had really come about—the finances of the Barrys, had better wait for another day.

"I need to borrow Dennis, here, for a little while, if that is all right with you," Dan said.

Richards gave Dan a piercing look.

Then he looked at the boy standing there in clothing a bit too small for him, although the green shirt and brown pants were clean.

"Everything all right?" Mr. Richards said. He obviously suspected something.

Dan had to give the kid credit for brains. He didn't attempt to lie. Instead, he just waited for Dan to answer.

Dan nodded.

"I'll just borrow him for a little while. I need to have him show me an area he is familiar with."

He didn't know why he had covered for the boy, but he had once again followed some gut instinct about what to do. The kid was an orphan. He had already had enough grief in his life, now he was living with people who were either indifferent to him or outright hostile.

But the kid was certainly no angel, either.

He followed Dennis, leading Sarah. The small boy had reddish-brown hair cropped very crudely and very, very short—Dan suspected it was to avoid the nuisance of having to give him frequent haircuts and to make washing his hair easier. But it looked as if someone had been angry when they cut it and taken their anger out with the scissors.

A wiry kid, he had a sprinkle of freckles across his nose

and cheeks, he looked surprisingly muscular for a kid his age.

He led Dan up away from the house and in about ten minutes Dan saw a level area of meadow hidden behind some trees.

He had to admit, what the kid had done was clever. Dennis had made a pen out of small-sized downed timber. He had laid the logs in a crisscross pattern similar to fences used by people in the Appalachians.

Dan didn't know the name of that kind of fence, but the logs were piled crisscrossing each other in short-ended X's. They were placed around to make a crude kind of low, tight corral.

Inside the corral three small goats were eating grass.

At the end of the corral, about thirty feet away, there was a small lean-to. A water bucket full of water stood near the doorway to the little shedlike building.

Climbing over the fence, Dan went to inspect the small crude goat house. In a corner, the boy had made a small bed out of logs and blankets which was obviously for himself. Straw was piled under the blankets to make a mattress of sorts.

The boy did not come inside. Instead he knelt by the goats and began talking softly to them and touching them gently. They were obviously used to his touch.

There was a bucket and a wet cloth in the corner. The boy was obviously milking the goats.

Probably the boy felt that these goats were the only living things in the world that loved him. He obviously loved them back.

There was only one problem.

He walked back over to Dennis and squatted beside him.

"It was wrong what you did."

"But she didn't love them like I do," Dennis said angrily.

"You don't own these goats. You stole them. Probably even stole the two water and milking buckets. Besides, Mrs. Nedlinger has her faults, same as the rest of us, but she does love these goats. They're like her babies. And she makes a living selling the goat milk and the goat cheese. She needs these goats."

He didn't think it was necessary to go into Mrs. Briggs's problems with a seven- or eight-year-old boy.

"What you did was wrong. Very, very wrong. I have a man in my jail right now for stealing. Do you want to end up like that?"

He almost said, "Don't you have enough problems already?" but he caught himself.

"Stealing is wrong. Don't you know that?" He added, "You can't just take what you want."

He thought for a minute.

"How did you get the goats here?"

Dennis walked back into the lean-to and came out with three small leather straps. Evidently they were small leads for the goats. He held the straps out so Dan could see them in answer to Dan's question.

He obviously knew that he was going to have to return them to Mrs. Nedlinger.

Dennis tied the leather straps carefully around each goat's neck and then helped Dan move some logs so that the goats could get out of the pen.

"You can herd them, but this is faster," Dennis said, sighing sadly. "We'll have to head to Mrs. Nedlinger's, right now, I suppose."

"You suppose right," Dan said very firmly. He let Dennis lead the way.

He felt odd to let the little boy lead the goats and for him to ride, so he walked behind the boy and the goats, leading Sarah. They made an odd group as they walked toward Mrs. Nedlinger's house: the boy, three goats, a man, and then a horse.

He would have helped the boy had he needed help, but Dennis seemed to have a way with the goats, and Dan thought it better if Dennis were made to return them himself. Dan was hoping the walk would give Dennis time to think about what he had done.

When they reached Mrs. Nedlinger's house, Dan called out, "Hallo the house."

He motioned to Dennis to go forward a bit toward the house with the goats.

She came to the door, and her face lit up. She hurried out of the door and rushed over quickly to greet them. She knelt beside the goats.

"Oh! Daisy! Freida! Marigold! I'm so glad to see you back. And you look fine and healthy! And I was so worried about you," Mrs. Nedlinger gushed.

She looked up at Dan, her eyebrows raised in question. Then she stood up. "Should I pay the boy something? Did he find them? Should I give him a reward?"

As she spoke, they looked, and the boy was gone, sulkily walking toward the pen that he had stolen the goats from, leading the goats.

"The boy is seven or eight. He lost his parents last year. He loves goats."

He lowered his voice. "Do you want to press charges? Or do you want to consider it a 'misunderstanding'?"

"He loves goats?"

"Even more than you," he said in a gently teasing manner.

They both watched how Dennis carefully returned the goats to their original pen, and gently removed the leather leads.

"Did you put the fear of God in him about stealing?"

"I think so. Maybe you'd better go over there and reinforce it. I talked more about jail than about God, Nellie, now that I think about it."

He sat there while Mrs. Nedlinger went over and talked to the boy. At first he was angry and sullen, but as she talked, after a while he began to bob his head up and down a lot. At the end of their talk, he seemed to be agreeing with whatever she was saying, and he handed the empty leather leads over to her.

Finally, they both came back over to him.

"Mrs. Nedlinger says that I can come over and visit her and the goats any time I want. She says that she is getting old, and she will even pay me if I help her with them. And pretty soon, she says that I could buy a baby goat from her and keep it here, *if* I keep my nose out of trouble and promise to give up stealing forever and ever."

Mrs. Nedlinger went up a couple of notches in Dan's opinion.

"It sounds like a good bargain to me. Keep you out of jail, for one thing. You a man of your word?"

The boy nodded yes. He seemed to be taking his promise seriously.

"Okay, then."

Relieved, as if a great load had been lifted from his chest, the boy turned and bobbed his head up and down in Mrs. Nedlinger's direction.

It was settled, then.

Suddenly, Dan was tired. He'd done enough for one day. He'd been up since before dawn. He'd have to return Dennis to the Richards, check back on Niles, then go home and check on Alister and tend his wound, and close the door to the barn after taking care of Sarah.

The finance inquiry would have to wait until tomorrow.

But at least Mrs. Briggs's milk supply was back here, safe.

Chapter Twelve

For the ride back to the Richards, Dan put Dennis up behind him on Sarah.

In a few minutes they were back at the Richards's home. As they rode up, Dan could see that Dennis's belongings were in a small pile outside of the house, on the narrow unpainted plank porch.

Mrs. Richards was the first out the door. She had obviously been furtively watching from one of the windows for their arrival. She looked as if she was ready for a confrontation.

Her arms were folded in a no-nonsense position over the front of her black dress.

Mr. Richards came out and looked at Dan.

''Stay on the horse,'' Dan said to Dennis, and he himself swung down off the horse. He and Mr. Richards, who seemed as if he would be the easier of the two people to deal with, went back and spoke under the big oak tree.

"I don't want to know what he's done," Mr. Richards started out saying. "And to tell the truth, I just don't care. There's been nothing but upset in this house since he arrived. I'm not saying it's all the kid's fault. She . . . they . . . don't get along, is all. Never did see eye-to-eye with her about it but it is just her way. I can't have her all upset all the time like she is. You'll have to take him."

He didn't give Dan a chance to argue back.

"It's done, now. It's for the best. Fact is, she resents him for still being alive when her own son is dead. Both our younguns is dead. But she was always attached special to the boy.

"It's my fault. I'm the one who brought him here. I thought it might help. Only it made things worse. I should have asked her first.

"Maybe if Dennis had been a girl it would have been different. I don't know. She's been actin' funny since . . . well, since they died. Anyways, take him with you. His stuff is on the porch. That's all I got to say. There's no use you arguin' about it."

Dan could see that there wasn't.

He strode back to the porch, picked up the pitifully few belongings, and then swung back up on the horse in front of Dennis. Dennis leaned back to allow Dan to seat himself.

On the way back to town both Dennis and Dan were quiet.

"What are you going to do with me?" a small voice said finally, from behind Dan's shoulder.

"We're going to stop at Pastor Cook's," Dan said.

"Life is not fair, you know that?" the small voice behind Dan's back said. "I just wanted the goats to be happy."

"I've found that it's best not to dwell on what's not fair about life," Dan said. "You just acknowledge it, and then get on with it. Otherwise, you can waste a lot of what otherwise would be good days."

But he looked down at the very small pile of belongings he was holding as they rode.

Chapter Thirteen

When they rode up to Pastor Cook's house next to the little white church building, the pastor came out of the front door. He walked over to where they were.

He looked up at Dennis on the horse in back of Dan, and Dan got the idea that the boy's arrival was not all that much of a surprise. In fact, he gave Dan a look of acknowledgment.

Dennis jumped down off the horse.

The pastor gave Dennis a warm welcome. Putting his arm lightly on Dennis's shoulder, he guided him toward the door.

"Come on inside, Dennis. Mrs. Cook has a nice supper on the stove. How about you, Sheriff? Would you like a bite to eat?"

Actually Dan would have enjoyed that a lot, but he had Alister and Niles to attend to yet.

''I hate to pass up your wife's good cooking, but I have a lot to do yet before I hit the sack this evening. Thanks anyway,'' Dan said.

Dennis had reached the door of the pastor's house before he realized that Dan still held his things. He came back and Dan handed him down the little bundle.

After the door had closed behind Dennis, Pastor Cook walked back over to Dan and said, ''Sorry it didn't work out at the Richards's. I feel sorry for the boy.''

''Will he be all right here with you?'' Dan said.

''My house is always open to those in need,'' the pastor replied. ''Missed you this morning in church,'' he added.

''Thanks, Pastor Cook,'' Dan said, relieved. He had his hands full right now, with Alister and with Niles. He said as much to the pastor.

The pastor hadn't heard about Alister's arrival in town, yet, so Dan told him, including the fact that the rumors had been wrong, and about Alister's bad leg.

The pastor didn't seem at all surprised that the rumors had been wrong. Then he said, ''Jay Garrity says that the robber doesn't seem like a bad sort. What do you think about Niles Olaf Turgstrom?''

''I don't know. Trial is a week from tomorrow, on a Tuesday morning. You going to be there?''

The question was just a formality. Pastor Cook always was.

''Yep. Same as always. You think you might feel the same as Jay about the robber?''

''I been thinkin' on it some,'' Dan admitted. ''We'll see what happens next Tuesday.''

As he rode away, it seemed to Dan that all he had been

doing lately was dropping people with no place to go at someone or other's house.

And Alister was at his own house, waiting for care.

As he rode back, the obvious thought was that Mrs. Nedlinger was the perfect match for Dennis Barry to live with. They had a lot in common. But Mrs. Nedlinger might not be any better than Mrs. Richards was for the boy. She might be too crochety. And those pretzels . . .

On the other hand, she had been remarkably understanding today about Dennis's problems.

Jay had done a good job at the office, so Dan rode on home. He hadn't meant to leave Alister so long. When he went inside his house, he was surprised to see Alister was up and about and had cooked supper for them both. Alister had fried up some bacon and eggs and potatoes, and Dan was glad to sit down and eat.

"Thanks, old-timer," he said gratefully as he dug in.

That night he was happy to lay his head down on the pillow after he had finished his chores.

The next morning, after doing his chores and then eating breakfast with Alister, he returned the mule to the livery stable to Jay who had just come across the street from the jail, and paid Jeff Graywood for use of the mule.

Jeff was unusually quiet, accepting the money with none of his usual good cheer. He seemed worried about something. Jeff was a man whose friendliness and willingness to share his last biscuit made him very well liked in town.

A tall, thin man, he had set out for the West when he was fifteen, leaving only a bachelor uncle. He'd lived with the uncle since his parents died when he was six. After he'd run away, he'd shined boots, peeled potatoes, sold newspapers, mined, prospected, and done other things before finally settling on running the livery stable in town. He had bought it with money he'd made prospecting in '49.

Dan considered him one of his best friends, but he hadn't seen much of him lately. Jeff had attended the funeral for Dan's mother and had packed the mule for him, but other than that both he and Dan had been busy lately.

Dan said, "Are you all right?"

Jeff nodded, and said, "Just tired, I guess."

Dan looked at him for a moment.

Why was he lying?

"If you need me, you know where I am," Dan said.

"Thanks, Dan," Jeff said, "but I'm all right."

Moments later, Dan walked back across the street to his office, but he had a feeling that something serious was bothering Jeff.

Mr. Richards showed up at the sheriff's office at eight-thirty, about a half hour after Dan arrived there. Niles was still asleep in the back cell. The blankets on Jay's cot were still rumpled; Jay had spent the night, as he usually did, when Dan had a prisoner. Sometimes, he and Jay took turns, but first Dan had been gone, and now he had Alister at his house, so Jay was sleeping on the cot every night.

Right now Jay was probably caring for the mule Dan had returned.

Richards walked in and began without any preliminaries, in a somewhat loud, hostile, defensive manner: "There was some confusion yesterday. My wife said that you told her you had come to talk about the boy's parents, the Barrys. Then you ran off with the boy suddenlike, and never mentioned to me what it was that you wanted to know about the boy's parents. . . . Is my wife mistaken about what you said, or what?'' Standing in front of Dan's desk, he was obviously ready for a scrap. He must feel guilty about how he and his wife had treated Dennis; he was definitely on the defensive, Dan thought.

Dan could feel himself growing hot under the collar; he needed to calm himself down. He forced himself to breathe in and out a few times before he answered. He'd had just about enough of the Richards's calling Dennis ''the boy,'' as if he had no name.

''Dennis?'' he said. ''Are you talking about Dennis?'' he said deliberately. ''Yes, I did want to talk to you about Dennis's parents.''

He gestured toward the chair.

''Sit, Mr. Richards.''

Richards sat unwillingly, but also unwilling to defy a sheriff's direct order. If that's what it was.

He let Mr. Richards squirm for a moment before he spoke. He also needed to calm his own temper down a bit. He wasn't the one who brutalized the boy's hair and kept him in too-small clothing and whupped him. And made him feel that nobody—except three small goats—loved him. And that he was no good.

And Dan was the one getting yelled at for all this, as if it was Dan's fault.

''What do you know about Enright and Maggie's financial status when they passed away?'' he said finally, when he had himself more under control.

''I know that if they'd left a little money, it would have helped us out a great deal in trying to care for the boy. As it was, it made a financial pinch, what with having to feed another hungry mouth. I'm not a rich man, you know.''

Dan nodded agreement, but he had no idea that the Richards had been in such a financial pinch with the addition of Dennis to the household. He assumed that the cattle business and the farm were enough to keep the Richards financially okay.

"If King had only sent us a bit, it might have helped soften Martha's attitude. Of course, we did our Christian duty by taking the boy in."

"That's what I'm asking you. Did Harvey King give you any money at all toward Dennis's upkeep?"

"No. None, not one penny. And we'd been under the impression—from the Barrys, of course—that they were better off financially than we were by a great deal. Money from back East, we'd heard, from Chicago. Cattle, I believe, and from not only Maggie's parents, but from a large estate that Enright had inherited."

"I had that impression, also." Dan said. So far, he'd not lost his temper and been very businesslike with Mr. Richards.

"What did Harvey King say about the Barrys's finances when he dropped Dennis off?"

"Weren't him that dropped Dennis off. I picked him up at the pastor's, remember? It was the pastor. . . . He was the one who told me that the Barrys didn't have no money left after their debts were paid. Said that Harvey King tole him that."

Richards thought a minute.

"I remember being surprised. Yep, I remember that very well, how *surprised* I was when I heard I wasn't going to get anything toward the boy's upkeep."

Richards had originally thought that he'd get money for taking "the boy" in, then. That was the real, main reason why he agreed to take him. That was becoming more obvious by the minute, more by his facial expressions than by what he said.

Richards started to stand up, anxious to go, then remembered that the sheriff had told him to sit. So he sat back down.

"What about the boy? What did you want him for yesterday? Can you tell me that? What did he do? Is he a *sinner*?"

Dan thought before he spoke.

"He showed me where some missing goats were." Technically that was not a lie. Again he found himself defending Dennis. Some stubborn part of himself didn't want to give Richards the satisfaction of saying "I knew the kid was no good from the moment I set eyes on him."

Maybe it would not be Eugene Richards saying it, maybe it would be his wife, Martha. But still, Dan did not want to give either of them the satisfaction. A picture was still in his head vividly of Dennis's brutal-looking haircut.

Mr. Richards's own haircut was neat and even.

Dennis's haircut was a haircut designed almost to make Dennis look bad.

He made up his mind at that moment.

If Dennis was "bad," the Richards would have had a "legitimate" reason to get rid of him, especially after they found out there would be no money.

"That's about it," Dan said to Mr. Richards. "That's all I wanted to know."

As he escorted Richards out, he called to Jay who was in sight out in front of the stable.

"Jay!"

Jay came over.

"Can you watch the office for a few minutes?" he said to Jay.

"Sure," Jay said, grinning.

"I've been thinking about something, Jay," Dan continued. "I need someone full time here, now. You interested? It would mean having to give up the part-time stable work."

He looked at Jay. Jay's thick, brown, curly hair always fell over the eyebrows on his pleasant-looking face. Jay was stocky and well muscled, although not as tall as Dan himself was. Jay grinned. "I been waitin' and hopin' that that would happen. If I never have to shovel out another stall I'd be a happy man."

"Great. It will be a little more than double your part-time wages. That okay with you?"

"More than great. Something I been lookin' forward to. Will I be your deputy, now?"

"Yes. You sure will."

"Deputy's badge and all?"

"We'll get you something," Dan grinned, as he swung up on Sarah, the leather creaking from the change in weight as he sat. "You can have the back room for your things. I hardly ever use it. From now on, I'll take that cot on nights I sleep here."

He pointed in through the open door to the cot just inside it on the left.

"I'll be back in a few minutes," he said to Jay.

Jay nodded happily, and went inside, probably to talk some more with Niles. They seemed to be getting to be close friends.

Dan rode over to the pastor's and dismounted. He went to the door.

The door opened as he approached the porch and the pastor came out, closing the door behind him.

"Howdy," the pastor said.

"How is Dennis doing?"

"Fine." the pastor said. "How is everything else going?"

"Moving along," Dan said. "I need to ask you something. I was talking to Eugene Richards about the Barrys. He admitted to being surprised that they had no money left after their funeral."

"So was I, more than a little," the pastor said. "But stewardship of money has always been something I'm not good at guessing about."

"What do you mean?" Dan said.

"Quite a few times I have been surprised, here in town, how many people had less than I imagined. I guess death costs and debts that need to be paid off keep going up."

"You mean that there were others? Others that you felt had more money than what Harvey King claimed?"

"Oh, my, yes." the pastor said, raising his eyebrows up. My wife and I discuss it quite a lot. Made us frightened for ourselves in our old age, if things cost that much. Oh, yes," he said, bobbing his head up and down in worry. "Death expenses. Made us worry quite a bit."

Death expenses? A pine box, a bit of white linen or cambric cloth sewed inside, and little else. A dollar-fifty for a pine box. People around here even brought food for the mourners. Families didn't even have to pay for food at a funeral. Death expenses?

‘‘Thanks, Pastor. By the way, I’d like to take Dennis for a few minutes, if you don’t mind. Into town, for a proper haircut.’’

The pastor seemed pleased with that, and in a few minutes, Dennis was up behind him on Sarah, going to town to the barber’s for a ‘‘proper’’ haircut.

Chapter Fourteen

After he paid for Dennis's new haircut—it was short, of necessity, because of the near scalping he'd gotten, at the hands of Mrs. Richards it turned out—Dan took Dennis to Ferd Cody's general store and bought him two new shirts, two new pairs of trousers, and socks and shoes, before he took him back to the pastor's house and dropped him off.

The barber assured Dan and Dennis that Dennis's hair would grow out just fine and in about two weeks Dennis would be looking great.

As he rode back to his office, he thought about Harvey King. If what he suspected about King was right, King was lower than a snake . . . lower and worse than an ordinary rattlesnake. At least a rattler usually gave you fair warning before he struck.

Jay had already fed Niles, so Dan walked up the street to Edna's Food Emporium to get a bite to eat.

As Edna served him coffee, buck stew and biscuits, he thought some more.

Harvey King preyed—a true vicious predator—on the helpless, much like a snake waiting in the shrubbery for a timid, trembling, whiskered, bright-eyed mouse.

King was about the same age as Alister, only about as different a man as you could get. Dan had never seen him disheveled or with a gray hair out of place. He was always impeccably clean and neat, well dressed in expensive materials most people could not afford. Ferd Cody ordered them special from the East, Dan had heard Ferd say, just for Harvey King.

To the townspeople, he cultivated the image of the perfect husband, a churchgoing man of God, a generous man.

Even Dan had never questioned it.

But Dan did know from previous experience, appearances are not always the truth. As both a human being and as a lawman, more than once he'd found that the person who put on the perfect face and appearance turned out to have a secret they were covering up—like vicious cruelty to family members in the privacy of their home, or some other equally dark secret.

The mask of perfection was deliberate so that no one would question the person and what they were doing. Only when a crack appeared in the mask would the secret behind it come out. If ever.

A person who made the lives of those around them a living hell. Was Harvey King a person like that?

It was true that Harvey had seemed to amass a great deal of wealth in the three years since Dan had been back in town. But he had never questioned a banker's ability to make a lot of money honestly.

But was he getting the money by stealing from his customers? Did his wife and family know?

How could Dan find out?

Often, the weak link was the family. If they were honest people, they might not be comfortable with his stealing. . . .

Meantime, his problems were mounting. What was going to happen to Niles?

What to do with Alister and his gold?

Where could Dennis stay? He couldn't stay with the pastor forever.

Where were Burt Black's chickens disappearing to? Who was stealing them?

And this new problem of his suspicions—which would be hard to prove—about Harvey King. What should he do about that? He paid Edna and left.

At his office everything was in order. Niles was lying on his cot, writing on a paper Jay must have given him. Dan guessed it was a letter home but he didn't ask.

He decided to take a ride out to Burt Black's and have a talk with him first.

Burt Black's ranch was not too far from the schoolhouse out past Julia Anderson's side of town. Burt and his wife and four children raised chickens for sale and also sold eggs to Ferd Cody at the general store.

Burt's wife sold live chickens, or, if requested, they killed, plucked and cleaned them—ready for the pot.

Often, the smell coming from the small house was not too pleasant. The plucking took place after the dead chicken was dipped in boiling water to make the plucking easier, but this procedure, as well as the next procedure—disemboweling the bird—stunk. Bad.

Chicken manure, also plentiful near the Blacks' farm, was not one of Dan's favorite smells. Not a pleasant aroma. But Burt sometimes sold the manure to farmers as fertilizer, so he had a different attitude toward it than most people.

Burt was walking from one of the chicken coops toward the house as Dan rode up. Curious, but not unfriendly, he strode with his large boots covered with chicken manure over to where Dan had pulled up on the reins to bring Sarah to a halt.

"You ready to sell that whistler?" Burt asked.

Burt was referring to a horse that wheezed, one with lungs that were no good. Some people called them horses that "couldn't keep a secret."

Dan grinned. "Not on your life."

It was a running joke.

Burt pretended to think that Sarah was a no-good horse and Dan should sell Sarah to him—"Take her off Dan's hands," he called it.

"Dying to get your hands on her, aren't you, Burt?"

"Just tryin' to do you a favor," Burt said, grinning. "Save you a bundle on feed. You don't want to have to feed an old broken-down horse like that too much longer."

Through with his teasing, he said, "What can I do for you, Sheriff?"

Dan swung down, carefully staying where he was, near a corral near the barn, and not going within sniffing distance—downwind—of the coops or house.

"Any more of your chickens missing?" Dan asked.

"Yes. A dozen or more disappeared since you've been

out here last. They've been disappearing out of my biggest coop."

"Got any idea as to what is happening to them?" Dan asked.

"Not any more than you do." Burt said, taking off his flat, black-rimmed hat, scratching his bald head, and then putting his hat back on.

"Wish I did. I'd empty my gun into the dad-blasted chicken thief if I had any idea who it was." Dan had an idea that Burt was only half joking.

"Well, until we find out who it is, I was wondering if you could do me a small favor and perhaps yourself a favor as well." Dan said. "I am getting busier and busier with the office. I don't have time anymore to take care of my chickens—they were really my mother's chickens. I was wondering if you would take them off my hands. I'd just as soon buy my eggs from Ferd Cody when I need them, as spend twice a day feeding and watering chickens, collecting eggs, and doing all the other things that need to be done."

He didn't need to mention shoveling manure out of the coop twice a month. Burt knew better than anyone the work that chickens took.

"How many you got?"

"About twenty-five or thirty, I'd guess. I haven't counted them in a while," Dan said. "Half price from what your usual price for a grown chicken's all I'd want for them. That and you come and get them yourself."

Burt looked pleased.

Burt knew a good deal when he saw one.

"Be out first thing tomorrow morning with my cages in my wagon," Burt said.

"My, ain't this town gettin' all citified, what with the sheriff gettin' so busy he ain't got no more time to take care of his own chickens and has to buy his eggs at the general store now," Burt teased, grinning.

"What you need is a wife. Too bad my children are all too young, or I'd be fixin' you up with one of my daughters. That way, I'd be the sheriff's father-in-law, and no one would *dare* sneak onto my property like they're doin' now.

"Dang chicken thieves! What peeves me the most is why I don't hear him when he comes? Why aren't they squawking?"

That was a good question.

Dan pondered it while he rode back to town. In this case, it wouldn't be a child like Dennis. This seemed to be methodical thievery, going on over a period of time. He'd have to spend a few nights out here, near the coop, watching. Burt had already been doing that, but so far, to no avail. Was the chicken thief feeding the chickens secretly so that the chickens knew him? That was the only solution that presented itself, so far.

The big chicken coop was set far back away from the house because of the smell. The thief was probably not a stranger. At least not to the chickens, Dan thought as he rode. Although a sleeping chicken . . . maybe someone was smart enough to grab the beak first so that it couldn't make noise. One chicken at a time . . . it could be done silently.

And chickens squabbled amongst themselves enough that even if the family had heard a small scuffling noise before the thievery began, they were likely to ignore it unless they thought an animal had gotten into the coop.

Back at the office, Dan unlocked a drawer and went

through a box left in his desk by the previous sheriff, who had tied his bedroll on his horse one morning shortly after Dan returned from the war and rode away. No one knew why. Tired of the job, Dan guessed. Or tired of being in one place too long.

Not long after that, a delegation from town had come out to his father's house and offered Dan the nomination, and he had been elected.

In the box was a new-looking deputy's badge. Dan left it on the desk where Jay could find it.

The next morning, he decided to go out and talk to Mrs. Nedlinger, to see if, one way or another, he could get it settled about Dennis.

He dreaded asking her. In fact, had been putting it off because if she didn't want Dennis he couldn't think of another family that would be willing to have him.

The town had its share of muleskinners, miners, farmers, prospectors, barroom owners, ranchers, cowboys, storekeepers, and various other businessmen, but few women. And few families able to take another child.

Julia was one of the few women in town who might have done it and he would have asked her, but he had already burdened her with Moira and Cassie. So she was out, at least for now.

Reluctantly, he set out for Mrs. Nedlinger's goat farm. Dennis would be at school, so it would be a good time for him to visit.

As he rode, a light, pleasant rain began to sprinkle down around him.

He adjusted his hat and reached around and grabbed the slicker behind him, unrolled it, and put it on as it began to rain harder. He guessed he couldn't complain, the weather had been extraordinarily good for a lot of days.

When he arrived, there was no sign of Mrs. Nedlinger outside. He dismounted, left Sarah nearby under the canopy of an oak tree and went and knocked on the door, and then stepped back.

Mrs. Nedlinger opened the door. She didn't seem surprised at his visit, except maybe that he had come in the rain.

''Put your horse in the barn and then come in.''

He did.

She stood on the porch waiting for him, watching. She seemed glad to have company.

''Come in,'' she said again, pleasantly, as he arrived back on the porch. She opened the door wide to allow him to follow her into her kitchen. He closed the door behind him, and took off his hat.

''Sit,'' she said, pointing to a chair near the table where she obviously had been standing, working with dough.

She took his slicker and hung it on a hook by the door.

Inwardly, Dan groaned.

She was making pretzels. . . .

He sat where she had indicated, hanging his hat on one of the knobs on the top of the back of the chair.

Her house was clean and neat, and surprisingly well furnished and decorated, with up-to-date things.

He would have thought from town gossip, that she was ''too cheap'' to spend this much money on fine furnishings.

Mrs. Nedlinger was a woman of surprises. As with Alister, he now suspected that town gossip was wrong about her, also.

''Have one,'' she said, pointing with floured fingers to

one of the huge batch of pretzels that had already been boiled and baked. It was not a small thin, twisted pretzel, but a sturdy brown, salt-speckled log, one-by-six inches long.

He took one, and as he bit it, he thought one of his teeth would break off, but the pretzel finally gave with a loud snap and his teeth were saved.

He chewed and chewed and chewed, dreading the next bite.

"What can I do for you," Mrs. Nedlinger said, deftly rolling another loglike shape as she talked.

"Uh," he said.

"Spit it out," she said, and for a moment he wondered if she meant the pretzel. Then he realized that she obviously meant for him to tell her what it was he had come for.

He sighed.

There was nothing to do but get right to it. He swallowed. He wished he had a drink of water.

"I have been doing a lot of thinking about Dennis," he began, inwardly cursing himself for this lame beginning.

"So have I," Mrs. Nedlinger said. "What was it that you were thinking?" she said, looking him right in the eye.

She had him pinned down.

He had to come right out with it.

"Dennis can't stay indefinitely with Pastor Cook and his wife," Dan began.

"And you were wondering if I would be dumb enough to take him?" she said bluntly.

"Well, I wasn't going to say dumb," Dan said, chuckling and grinning at her.

"He's a handful, that kid." Mrs. Nedlinger said. "He's stubborn and willful. Needs strong moral guidance. He'd ride roughshod over anyone meek."

Dan nodded. The kid was strong willed. She was right.

"You sayin' you think *I* should take him?"

"The thought had occurred to me," Dan said grinning. He was relieved that she was at least thinking about it, the same as he was.

"I'm not sayin' I will," Mrs. Nedlinger said. "But I will say I will ponder on it some.

"I want you to be honest with me," she said.

"Have been so far," Dan said in a joking manner.

"Dennis tells me that nobody likes my pretzels. Is that true?"

"I'd have to say he's pretty much right about that," Dan said, tactfully lowering the uneaten pretzel below table level so that she couldn't see it.

"I'm alone out here, and it makes me happy to make them," Mrs. Nedlinger said. "My mother made them. It brings back happy memories to me when I make them, and it helps my rheumatism some to use my hands this way," she said, rolling another chunk of pretzel dough into a log.

"Of course, I don't make them as good as she used to," she added regretfully. "Mine are harder than hers. I don't know why."

She finished that pretzel, laid it aside, and began forming another one, then she stopped and thought.

After a minute she said, "How about doughnuts? What if I made doughnuts instead? Would that be better?"

Dan had eaten her doughnuts at church socials. They were good. Not greasy and heavy, but fried right, just about perfect.

"Yes," he said, "that would be great."

Dan looked out the kitchen window. The rain was pouring down very hard now.

"Guess I better be going now," he said as he stood up.

"Here, give me that pretzel," Mrs. Nedlinger said kindly, but a little embarrassed, as he stood up and went to get his slicker to put it back on. He gave it to her.

He put his slicker and hat back on, said good-bye, and left.

He was glad that the talk had gone as well as it had.

Mrs. Nedlinger had been very friendly as she said good-bye.

More and more he thought that Mrs. Nedlinger and Dennis were a good match. He was hopeful.

The rain was beginning to make mud. Sarah's hoofs splashed mud and water upwards. As he rode to town he realized that he'd forgotten to ask Mrs. Nedlinger about Harvey King. That could wait until he saw her next, he guessed. One thing at a time, for now. He had made progress on Dennis's future, he hoped. Besides, he didn't want to alert Harvey King too soon that he was interested in his present and past activities. Before he had proof, if there was any, of Harvey King's wrongdoings.

When he got back to the office, the money from the sale of his chickens was on his desk, left there by Burt Black.

The rain kept people inside until Friday night so it was quiet. Jay slept in the room in the back office and Dan went home nights. Alister was doing fine, and helped Dan with the livestock and cooking.

Dan stayed in his office late Saturday night. It had rained very heavily and even though it had turned to just a light, steady drizzle near dusk, enough had fallen so that the street was a solid sea of mud about three to four inches deep, and it had been churned up by every boot, hoof, and wagon wheel that had passed through it. The mud was almost as bad as it was during the rainy season in the winter, when it would be mostly rain here below but deep snow falling on the tops of the high mountains.

Worse, this rain had kept people indoors, and more than a few had been "bending their elbows" in the four saloons all day, during the storm. It was the reason Dan had stayed in town tonight. He was glad Alister seemed to be doing fine lately. He was perky and peppy, and able to care for his own wound now.

It was Ferd Cody who rushed into Dan's office around ten o'clock, his breath smelling strongly of whiskey.

"Sheriff, come quick! Come quick! There's a big fight going on in Big Alice's saloon! The Cornish and the Dutch miners got into a fight! And the Irish miners joined in, for no apparent reason!"

Dan hurried, following Ferd's dash out into the foggy darkness. The rain seemed to be letting up, but his boots sunk deep into the mud as he squished his way through it to Big Alice's saloon.

As he crossed the middle of the street, he heard two gunshots. Sounded like revolvers.

He reached the door and went in, mud dripping and plopping off his boots as he entered. Inside, just as Ferd had said, there was a big brawl going on. Eight or nine men were fighting. Fortunately, Big Alice had long ago given up on mirrors in back of the bar. Instead, she had a collection of grizzly bear hides tacked on that wall.

Big Alice was a big woman who tended to smell mighty strong on a hot day. People didn't usually mess with her or her saloon. A big, buxom blond, tonight she had on a pink silk low-cut dress with glittering black beads sewn on around the sleeves and collar, and long black glittering earrings. The dress looked new.

The bartender, a man equally as large as Alice named Captain John, was yelling at the men fighting, trying fruitlessly to break up the fight. He was standing between two of the men punching, trying to stop them.

Captain John's hat, usually on his head, was on the floor, knocked off and being stepped on, and maybe ruined, by muddy boots. There was mud clinging to it. He must be angry about that, Dan knew.

One man mistakenly punched Captain John, as he got in the way of the man punching someone else, and Captain John punched the man back as Dan entered.

They were destroying the place. Chairs had already been flung about and broken, probably some from hitting people, Dan guessed.

Tables were overturned.

Broken bottles and glasses were on the floor in front of the bar and elsewhere.

The men froze as Dan entered.

One man had a bloody nose. Two had ripped shirts, and another was pressing a neckerchief over a bleeding cut over his eye.

Dan was surprised.

Dan felt, rather than saw that Ferd had entered the saloon and stood behind him.

Tensions must be high. Both the Dutchmen—some of them Germans but called "Dutch" or Dutchmen—and the Cornishmen were usually well-behaved citizens, not troublemakers at all.

In the corner of the room with his back to the wall, stood

one obviously drunken German miner, his pistol in his hand.

"He shot at me," one of the Cornishmen yelled to Dan as Dan entered the saloon.

"He shot at me!" the Cornishman repeated, shouting as he pointed at two bullet holes in the floorboards of the saloon near his boots.

"Did you?" Dan inquired.

The man looked unrepentant but scared now that the sheriff had arrived.

"Ya," the man said, lowering his gun. "I never meant to hurt him," he said. "Yust teach him a lesson on manners," he said, walking toward Dan and lowering his gun so that the butt faced up and the barrel faced downward toward the floor. Dan took the pistol from the man's outstretched hand.

"He said I drank as much as Murphy, here. I said that's a durn-blasted dang lie. I don't . . . and he said I did, and we got to goin' at it an' I yust got carried away is all."

A bunch of heads bobbed simultaneously in agreement. "We yust got carried away is all." No one was eager to spend the night in jail.

Big Alice already had a paper out, writing down who broke what. They were going to pay for what they had broken, if she, herself, had to lift them up, turn them upside down and shake them to empty out their pockets. And they all knew she could, especially with Captain John's aid.

"You take him," she said, indicating the shooter who had given Dan the gun. I'll handle the rest of them."

The men grinned, choosing to take what she had said in a profane way.

The man handing the gun to him knew his fate. He

sighed, and walked over to Dan, resigned and ready to spend the night in jail.

He did.

Dan released him in the morning, hangover and all. The man walked across the street to pay Big Alice for the bullet hole damage to the wooden plank floor.

But during his time in the cell, he said that the mining company had lowered all their pay by fifty cents a day. That was what the tension was really all about.

Gossip was even floating around that the mine was to be closed in six months, the man said. The big stampers—the rock crushers—would soon be quiet at the mine five miles away to the north, in an area noted for red dirt that clung to your skin, even after you had washed with soap and water.

They worked in an area of red ledges and red gravel, famous from earlier Gold Rush days for its rich deposits of gold. Word was that the owner had taken $400,000 out of the area in the last few years.

But gossip was, the strike was petering out.

Chapter Fifteen

At church on Sunday, there were a few surprises. First, Alister, who appeared to be getting better every day, insisted on going. To Dan's surprise, he appeared clean-shaven and well-dressed, ready to go when Dan came out of his own bedroom dressed for church.

Being clean-shaven took ten years off his looks, and made him look more vulnerable than the look his previous, tough-looking miner's beard had given him.

Dan lent him a dollar to put in the basket so as to not arouse suspicion about his having gold.

When they entered the church and went to sit down, Alister abruptly left his side and went and deliberately sat right in the pew in front of Harvey King, so that Harvey would have to stare at the back of Alister's head all through the service.

Mrs. King, next to her husband, was a softly disheveled

woman, who always looked as if she was worried about something. Her eyebrows were always slightly knit as if she had a little headache. Their two children, a boy and a girl, were almost completely grown adults. They were not in church this morning.

Mrs. Nedlinger was next to Julia, Cassie, and Moira.

Dennis, having no family to sit with, left Mrs. Cook's side as they entered, and came and slid into the pew, sitting next to Dan.

Mr. and Mrs. Richards entered, and acknowledged Dennis and Dan with the slightest faint suggestion of a nod and then proceeded to a seat two rows up, directly in front of Dan and Dennis.

As they sat, Mrs. Richards leaned over and picked a piece of lint off the shoulder of Mr. Richards's black suit jacket.

Something his father had once said to Dan in jest popped into his mind. His father had said, "Never marry a woman who picks lint off you in public." He said it at a Sunday church social after looking at one of the other couples there.

Now, Dan thought that he knew what he meant. He was always slightly irritated if a woman picked lint off him. It had happened only rarely, but for some reason it was slightly insulting.

Horace Blackthorn was there, glaring at Cassie, Moira and Julia for some reason, a big scowl on his face. But the biggest surprise was Cassie. She was casting glances over at Alister as if she was looking at the most handsome man in the world.

Alister? A ladies man?

Even Julia looked a few times at Alister with interest.

Well, nothing surprised Dan much anymore. And Alister

had certainly been very loyal and attached to his first wife. A good husband.

But it was Cassie that seemed to be the most obviously interested; she seemed oblivious to their age difference. Well, to quote his father again, he used to say that in the romance department there was a shoe for every foot.

Dan wondered who in the congregation the parson had in mind this Sunday; the sermon was on ''Forgive Us Our Trespasses.''

Outside, after the service, Cassie came over to where Alister and Dan were standing, where Dan usually stood after the service, under the oak tree.

That way, people who wanted to tell him something knew where to find him. He made himself available for people who were shy about coming to the office. Sometimes, here, they might mention something that was bothering them.

Cassie walked over holding Moira's hand, and Dan made introductions.

''My, my,'' Cassie said to Alister, obviously flirting. ''You've quite a reputation in town. I was so glad to hear that those nasty rumors weren't true. I can tell by looking at you . . .'' Her voice trailed off, her point made and taken well by Alister.

''I'm a widow,'' Cassie added. Alister seemed pleased by this news and Dan would be darned if the older man didn't stand up straighter and seem to lose even a few more years in the process.

''Perhaps you might drop in and visit me and my daughter at Julia's here, after church, and tell us of your adventures.'' Cassie said smoothly. ''If that is all right with Julia, of course,'' she said, looking for approval at Julia.

Julia said to Alister, "Certainly."

Julia looked over at Dan, a secret smile seeming to come both from her eyes and her lips, as if she was inwardly chuckling at how Cassie and Alister seemed to be mutually admiring each other.

About one o'clock, Alister walked into the sheriff's office where Dan was sitting. He was too excited to even sit down and rest his leg.

"Me and Cassie talked it all over. I tole her everything. I'm going to take my gold, turn it into cash money in Red Bluff, and open a bank here in town. A *good* bank. An honest bank! That ought to fix Harvey King but good!"

Chapter Sixteen

By three o'clock, Sunday afternoon, Dan also knew the reason for Horace's ill humor in church: Crooked Charlie's idea was a success. In fact too much of a success, as far as Horace was concerned.

Students from Horace's school had begun to appear at Cassie's new school in the Morris house, which was on the road out of town, just before the turn-off to go to Mrs. Nedlinger's and the Richards's houses.

Cassie was a good, kind teacher. Her students began coming home spouting new facts and interesting information which impressed their parents. Some of the information was such that the parents didn't know it themselves, like who the king of England was, and the dates when different states had joined the Union, and things like that.

Pretty soon Horace had only three students left, and Cassie had fifteen.

Horace went through the roof.

He'd been teaching in town for twelve years.

In a huff, he'd devised a plan to get his students back. He came up with the idea and presented it to Cassie, Ferd Cody, Harvey King, Pastor Cook, and the parents of the students that had bolted over to Cassie's school.

His plan was this: The students who had bolted were to come back for three weeks. At the end of that time both sets of students were to take a test. As he was planning to have his students be the ''winner'' as the tests were scored, he was sure that the parents would then return him his students permanently.

Prizes were to be awarded to students achieving the top three scores on the test.

The test was to be on Greek mythology.

Cassie could not refuse.

Ferd Cody agreed to donate the prizes, and the teaching was to begin Monday.

Monday, Dan was busy with other things. Tuesday was Niles's trial. Dan also had a lot of other things he was working on—other irons in the fire, so to speak.

Early Monday morning, he spoke to the new owner of the blacksmith's shop, who had bought it from the judge when he retired. Dan was given permission to go up in the loft and he and Jay Garrity dragged the large box full of records to the edge of the loft, and then struggling, got it down the ladder. After that, they carried the heavy box to the sheriff's office.

Looking through a giant pile of old, seemingly unsorted

papers was not a chore that Dan liked. Jay stayed in the office tending to Niles and fussing around, anxious to be of help. But Dan wanted to do the reading himself. At least he thought he did, at first.

It took a lot of time, reading writing that was often difficult to decipher, at best, and at worst misspellings and odd spellings of words that made it even more difficult. Some people used *f*'s for *s*'s, and other odd variations. Southerners tended to spell as they pronounced things and Northerners did the same.

He did find one paper for which Harvey King would have to come up with a good explanation. It was a deed for a large parcel of property that was to go to Edith Raines Maxwell in the event of her parents' deaths.

There was another paper verifying receipt of some money that had come to the judge to be given to Robert Raines Maxwell, an inheritance from his parents in Chicago. The amount was twenty thousand dollars, and the judge was evidently acting as a lawyer, at that time, for the Maxwell family. It was before the judge bought the blacksmith's shop and had changed careers, Dan guessed. In any case, he appeared to be acting as a lawyer on the Maxwells' behalf.

It seemed to support Alister's case.

What had happened to the money and the property?

He showed Jay the papers he had found, talking softly up near the desk in the front of the office so that Niles wouldn't hear.

''Whoa,'' Jay said quietly. ''Harvey must have collected a bundle on that one.''

Dan was surprised that Jay didn't seem surprised.

''Never liked King. Always thought he got rich too quick

for around here,'' Jay said. ''His wife is nice, though,'' Jay said.

''Got a favor to ask of you,'' Dan said. ''Keep all of this under your hat until I finish checking Harvey out.''

''Sure,'' Jay said. ''Got a favor to ask of you. Need Thursday and Friday off, if that is all right with you. Want to drive Alister over to Red Bluff on an *errand,''* he said, letting Dan know by his manner that errand meant bringing Alister's gold there to be exchanged for money, and that he didn't want anyone to overhear their plans.

Dan said, ''That would be fine. You going to take him in your wagon?''

''Yep.''

''Got some barrels that need to go to Red Bluff,'' Jay said more loudly.

The gold, then would be hidden in barrels on the way to Red Bluff.

''That would be fine,'' Dan said, signaling his approval.

He read more of the paperwork in the trunk, struggling his way through the difficult-to-understand papers. He was coming across more and more questionable activities regarding Harvey King.

A bank in town had been robbed—and put out of business—by armed and masked bandits a month before Harvey arrived in town to open his bank. He was greeted by the townspeople as a savior of sorts.

Now, Dan wondered if there was some connection between the two things. It did seem like a strange coincidence that King arrived to start a new bank just when the old bank . . . Hadn't Harvey even bought the same building the old bank was in?

What was the other name he was looking for? K. G.

James? He began to look for papers with the first name beginning with a K. and James as a last name. Relatives of K. G.

It took a long time. The papers were in a mess. He couldn't seem to find any system that they were filed under. They weren't in chronological or alphabetical order.

They were just jumbled together.

Finally, he found a paper that seemed to indicate that K. G.'s parents had owned—free and clear—property east of town. A small farm. It had been sold to the Lee family a year after K. G.'s parents died, he thought he remembered from town gossip.

Who did they pay the money for the land to? Could they have paid it to Harvey King?

Evidently people had dug through these papers over the years, and not put them back in order.

What else was hidden in these papers? Perhaps this trunk was the *one thing* Harvey King had either overlooked in his plans or not known about. In fact, there was no reason why he should have known about these papers since Judge Brown and Harvey King had never gotten along. There was no reason that the judge would have mentioned these papers to Harvey King.

But Judge Brown and his own father had been close friends. That was the only reason Dan knew about the papers. He'd heard the two men talking.

Dan suspected that one of the reasons that he had been selected to run for sheriff in the first place was that the judge liked him. He had known Dan for years, and was one of the few people who knew just what it was Dan had done during the war. It was not something Dan wanted known.

He had been transferred from the cavalry and reassigned to be a sharpshooter, picked for sniper duty by Colonel Hiram Berdan. Berdan led a corp of sharpshooters.

He sent lone sharpshooters to pick off Confederate generals during battles. From experience with Berdan's group Dan had come to favor, as had the rest of the sharpshooters, a plain dull gun without any ornamentation to shine in the sunlight and attract the enemy's attention. Not even the slightest bit of raised work—decorations—that could spoil his aim.

He had been given a bench rifle. It weighed thirty pounds and accounted for the muscles he had now in his upper body and shoulders. The rifle required him to sit or lay prone beside a special bench. It was a slow procedure to load, adding to the tension in being a sniper close to the enemy. He'd had to measure the charge, trim the ball, center it, adjust the long telescopic sight, adjust for the wind or other conditions, cock the hammer, place a cap on the nipple, look through the sight, pull the first set of triggers, stop to check his aim, and then, only then, when his gray-suited target was on *dead center,* would he fire. Only he and a few others knew which southern generals he had killed. . . . It was a terrible thing that he had to live with. It had been a sobering experience.

As a sheriff now, he was careful not to get a reputation as a fast draw. He didn't want to have to go against drunken young men trying to get a reputation. And he always tried to bring people back alive to be tried by a judge or jury. It was a thing of honor with him. So far, since the war was over, he'd never had to shoot anybody. He hoped he'd never have to again.

Dang! He had to stop thinking about what was in the past, and get back to studying these papers!

He had to give up, start over, and spread the papers out on the desk, floors, and chairs, frustrated as all get-out. Finally, he had them in order by the dates. There were so many names on some of the papers that going by names alone was too confusing. If he expected to make any sense out of these papers, it would take weeks. A person's name might appear on twenty papers, under different dates, for different things. He'd almost have to list names in chronological order, on a piece of paper.

Harvey would have apoplexy if he knew what Dan was finding in these papers!

They seemed to end—the most recent dates—about the time that Judge Brown retired. That was about two years ago. More current records were at the new judge's house.

He looked over at Niles, sleeping.

Jay had left without saying where he was going as Dan was busy reading. He had obviously not wanted to disturb Dan.

Dan gathered up the papers earliest dates first, then gathered up the later and later papers. He put them all back into the trunk—except for the ones which had names on them that included Barry, James, and Maxwell—and locked them in the empty cell, in the far back corner so that no one could get them. The Barry, James, and Maxwell papers—he unbuttoned his shirt, tucked them inside, and rebuttoned his shirt.

Niles, used to having Dan or Jay move about the office, never stirred in his sleep. Niles had been doing an awful lot of sleeping.

Without locking the office, he walked down to Edna's

and ordered ham, eggs, toast and coffee for Niles, and returned with it and put it down outside the bars of Niles's cell for his lunch.

Niles was still asleep.

He locked the door. Jay would be back in a minute. He was either at the stable or the outhouse, Dan guessed.

Then Dan left for the short walk to the old, retired judge's house.

When he reached the house, which was two houses up the street from Julia's, he knocked.

Judge Brown came to the door, using his cane. His white hair was perfectly parted in the center and combed to the sides. He was dressed in a clean white cotton shirt and a neat black suit.

The judge walked into the old parlor, sat down slowly, and then waved his hand toward a chair, indicating that Dan should sit. He did.

Dan lost no time telling the old judge every single thing he knew, and thought, and suspected about Harvey King, then he got up and gave him the papers he had inside his shirt. The judge, though old, was still sharp as a new razor. With a practiced eye, he glanced quickly through the papers Dan had given him.

"These are serious charges and accusations," the judge said. "I'll see what I can find out, and if I find anything, I'll get in touch with Judge Herbert. You can be sure of that."

"Do you want to see the rest of the papers that are in the chest?" Dan said.

"Might as well. Need to refresh my memory after all these years. They were my doings—my own paperwork—but it's been a while."

There was probably no one in town Dan trusted more than he did this old, respected man. If there was anything, Judge Brown would find it.

"And you can be sure, if I do find anything, I'll take it to Judge Herbert. There's no flies on him. He'll take care of things in short order."

That was true, the new judge was nothing if not noted for *not* being a dawdler.

Dan could see that Judge Brown was eager to study the papers that Dan had given him as well as those that remained in the chest. Within the hour, he and Jay had used Jay's wagon to transport the chest of papers to the judge, who would be able to make a lot more sense of them than Dan had. It was a relief for Dan. Paperwork was not something he enjoyed, but something that Judge Brown obviously did.

Chapter Seventeen

Tuesday morning at five of nine, Dan unlocked the cell door and walked Niles to a vacant building that used to be a general store that had gone out of business.

Jay had fed Niles at seven-thirty although Niles, too nervous to eat, had just drunk his coffee and left the rest of the bacon, eggs, and biscuits uneaten.

Jay accompanied Niles and Dan, quietly trying to reassure the frightened man as they walked the short distance down the same side of the street, past the two saloons, and past Edna's Food Emporium, to the vacant store where the trial was to be held.

As they arrived, they saw that many people were already gathering there. Someone, probably Ferd Cody had unlocked the door earlier and set up a table against the side wall to the left, and a bunch of chairs. Behind the table sat one chair—for the judge. And a chair prominently displayed in the center of the room was for Niles. One chair was off to the side, for Jay. Ferd knew that Dan would stand near the door, ready to act if there was any trouble.

Dan escorted Niles inside, and Niles walked over and sat in the chair.

The room was already crowded, as was the porch outside, which was an indication that people had gotten up real early to attend to their livestock and do morning chores so they could be here at this hour.

Among the rough clothing of the people at the far back of the room, between the shoulders of men and women crowded there, Dan saw a familiar face.

Saying "Take care of him," to Jay, Dan left Niles and walked over to Dennis, who was trying to squirm behind the backs of broad-shouldered men to get out of sight of Dan.

"What are you doing here, young man," Dan said, as he outmaneuvered him and came face to face with Dennis.

"I wanted to find out . . ." he paused.

"You wanted to find out what was going to happen to the man who stole?" Dan said, completing the sentence that Dennis had started and been embarrassed to finish.

" 'Member you tole me about him? The man in your jail? Is that him?" Dennis asked, looking with great concerned interest at the worried-looking Niles sitting on his prominently placed, isolated chair.

"That's him," Dan said. "Robbed Ferd Cody."

"He goin' to get the hangman's knot around his neck?"

"We'll have to wait and see on that," Dan said. "Some places, yes, without question. Here, we're pretty modern. We'll have to wait and see."

The new judge was quite a character.

Dan remembered two months ago when there had been a shoot-out where the gunman who had both started it and had drawn first had been killed in Crooked Charlie's saloon by Elliot Graham. The judge had come in, walked to the back of the table and had spoken very loudly: "There ain't no need to clutter my records with idiot cases of self-defense. Case dismissed!" he yelled as he banged his gavel down and walked back out the door. He'd been in the room less than one minute.

The last Dan had seen of Elliot Graham was him riding down the street towards the east—toward the mountains—with his bedroll behind his saddle—a sign that he was high-tailing it out of town, probably permanently, since the dead man had a lot of brothers.

Another time the judge had come in, and yelled, "There will be no *bullyragging* today; I got a bad headache!" And there was no bullyragging in court that day—no bullying, insulting, or intimidating with noisy threats.

The judge was notoriously fair, but also a man that did not tolerate what he called "highfalutin nonsense" in his courtroom. He was apt to threaten those who were too wordy in the courtroom, "I rile mighty easy!"

It was amazing how quickly people got right to the point in Judge Herbert's courtroom.

"Dennis, you should be in school," Dan said, at the same time, understanding Dennis's interest in the case, seeing that he and Niles had something in common. Theft.

"You're liable to get ten or twenty smacks with the ruler on your palms for this from Mr. Blackthorn."

"I know," Dennis said. It seemed to be a price he would be willing to pay to find out what happened to Niles.

Maybe it wouldn't hurt for the boy to see what trouble stealing brought you, Dan thought to himself.

He wiped the sweat off his brow. It was getting awfully hot in the small room; so many people were squeezed in there together, there was hardly room to move. Practically every adult he knew was there. He had to get back to Niles.

"You go to school as soon as this is over," he said sternly. "I'm going to check to see if you do," he said.

Dennis nodded.

"Dang, it's getting hot in here," Dennis said. "It's so hot my freckles are sweating right off me," he said, wiping his nose and face off with his shirttail, which he had just pulled out of his trousers.

Dan made his way back—people retreated to let him through—to where Niles sat, and then Dan went and stood near the door in a prominent place, waiting for the judge to arrive.

Usually the judge made an impressive sight as he arrived. He was aware of the power of the drama in a courtroom and Dan always felt that he knew that being intimidating was part of his job. He and Dan had discussed it on occasion.

Today, though, the judge arrived in such a state that Dan couldn't believe it. Neither, evidently, could any of the other usual spectators. Judge Herbert was a mess and had obviously been either crying or close enough to it that a person looking couldn't easily tell the difference.

For a moment, Dan wondered if the judge was drunk. But he wasn't a drinker. Upon looking closely, he saw that it was not liquor but some tragedy that had struck the judge, and recently enough that he had not had sufficient time to warn Dan about it and cancel or put off the trial.

Judge Herbert walked behind the table and put his double-barreled shotgun where he always put it—right behind his chair, leaning the shotgun up against the wall. He pulled the table closer to the wall after he sat down so that he was still in easy reach of his shotgun, as he usually did.

He drew some crumpled papers out of his coat and unfolded them and put them on the table in front of him. They were the papers Dan and Ferd had given him about the theft.

Gossip was spreading rapidly through the courtroom, and reached Dan just about the time that the judge was settled in his chair. A gavel was on the table to his right, where Ferd had put it.

Ferd Cody came over and whispered in Dan's ear.

The news *was* shocking. Jeff Graywood and the judges's wife, Jenny, had run off together this morning. When the judge had gotten up at seven-thirty, there was a note on his kitchen table instead of coffee and breakfast.

By an hour after dawn, they had been long gone; Jeff abandoning his livery stable and Jenny abandoning the judge, who was fifteen years older than she was.

The note didn't say where they were going.

Dan walked over to Jay. "Do you know anything about this?" he whispered.

"No." Jay whispered back, looking surprised himself. "I can't hardly believe it!"

The judge looked as if this was the worst day of his life as indeed, Dan thought, it probably was if what he had heard whispered to him was true.

"Order, Gentlemen!" Judge Herbert said loudly, but in a choked up voice, banging the gavel down firmly on the table.

There was immediate quiet in the crowded room, except for one thing the crowd had no control over: The judge had the hiccups. Probably from crying, Dan thought.

"This here court *(hic)* is called to order *(hic)* on account of thievery . . . No, actually outright face to face *(hic)* robbery," he said, reviewing his papers in front of him.

Dan stepped forward.

"Judge, do you want to postpone?" Dan asked politely.

"Not on yer *dang* life," the judge said, hiccupping one more time. "Let's git this over with!"

He nodded approval to a woman who had hurried in the door with a tin cup full of water and handed it to the judge. He took a sip and then nodded approval again at her kind deed.

"In this court, we are known far and wide for our fairness," he began again, "and it's a shame that it takes a harsh lesson, sometimes, to teach a man something that he should have learned earlier in his life: 'Thou shalt not steal' . . . and that includes," he said, his blue eyes sternly looking directly in the eyes of Niles Olaf Turgstrom, "stealing from Ferd Cody."

He paused.

It was quiet in the court. He turned and looked at Ferd.

"So, Ferd, is this the man that stole from you?"

"Yes."

"How much?"

"Twenty-three dollars and forty-seven cents."

"You get it back?"

"Yes. The sheriff caught Mr. Turgstrom and brought him back. He was took mountain sick. Puked and run at both ends."

"You got anything to say for yerself?" the judge said, looking back at Niles.

"No, no," Niles stuttered, almost crying.

"Well, it seems, here, that we *both* are having a hard day today," he said, taking note of Niles's tears.

"Does this man have any friends here in court that will speak for him?"

Jay stepped forward.

"Me, yer Majesty . . . I mean your Honor."

The judge accepted this without comment, except to look at the new deputy's badge pinned on Jay's clean blue and white checkered shirt.

He turned back to Ferd Cody and Dan, and his shoulders sagged. He gave out one big tired sigh and then said to them: "well, I heard about enough. Figure this out yerselves. It addles my brain today what to do. He ain't a murderer or dang hoss thief. . . . He ain't a merciless killer. . . . He ain't paid off witnesses to say he ain't done it. My suggestions is this . . ."

The judge interrupted what he was about to say and turned back and stared hard at Niles and said sternly, "Yer durn lucky I'm feelin' the way I do today. You might have gotten the noose an' *(hic)* been made a tree decoration if I was my usual self."

Then he turned and continued to Ferd and Dan. "As I said, my suggestions is this: Ferd, you get to pick, onct you've talked it over with Dan, here. One, punish this man with stripes."

He meant a whipping.

"Lash, whip, rod, or strap. I recommend twenty or twenty-five. Mebbe twenty-three, same as the money.

Flogged in public on his bare back for all to see the marks of the lash as a warning of what happens if you steal.''

He paused for that to sink in, and then he added, ''Next, he be made to pay back double, or triple what he stole, to teach him a lesson on the fruitlessness of stealing.''

He looked at Niles, and then said, ''Or third, banishment. Leave town immediately, forever. And never show yer face in this area again. Ever.''

''Order, gentlemen!'' he said, loudly at the murmur that had sprung up at his unusually lenient suggestions.

He looked again at Niles, sternly.

''You be thankful that justice is doled out quick in River Grove. You didn't spend months in jail awaiting trial, or months after it.''

He was admitting it was necessary for a trial to come quick here, Dan knew, as did all the others, except for possibly Niles himself. A delay meant witnesses might have moved on, been killed, died, or disappeared.

''Niles Olaf Turgstrom, let this be a lesson to you and all that are here,'' the judge thundered, recovering somewhat. Now that he was into it his hiccups seemed to have disappeared.

Dan looked over at Dennis. Dennis's eyes were wide open and his eyebrows were raised as if he thought that the judge was speaking to him personally.

''An evil man has only strangers to bury him. A man who is careless of morals and is dissolute comes to a bad end. Court has ended.''

He picked up the gavel and slammed it down on the table. Stunned people stayed to turn to each other and talk. The judge got up, stuffed the papers back in his coat pocket, turned, picked up his shotgun, and was gone before Dan could reach him.

The judge had never done anything like this before.

Dennis slipped out the door right behind the judge, looking at Dan to make eye contact to reassure him that he was going to school, then Dennis was gone out of sight of the store window.

Ferd, Jay, and Dan gathered around Niles, who sat as if unable to move or comprehend what had happened.

''Well that was that,'' Jay said. ''What'll we do now?''

''Go over to the office and talk this over,'' Dan said, looking at Ferd for confirmation. It was Ferd who was to make the final decision.

''We got to think on this for a bit, Sheriff,'' Ferd said, worried. He was a fair man, and this was a big responsibility. The townspeople would all be watching what he did. To be too lenient was to invite more robberies. Dan understood the dilemma this court decision posed for Ferd.

He touched Ferd's shoulder for a second to reassure him that he would help him think this through.

Chapter Eighteen

Back at the office, Dan sent Jay across the street for coffee for all of them. Niles sat outside of his cell for the first time. He was on the cot against the wall, opposite the desk. Dan sat in the chair behind the desk and Ferd sat in the chair in front of the desk. They talked softly so that Niles could not hear. If he did hear them, he gave no appearance of it, he just stared out the window. Dan knew Niles was relieved that he would not be facing the hangman's noose this morning.

"So what do you think?" Dan said.

"I don't know," Ferd said. "I got to think on this some. I'm not sure I like what the judge did."

Dan agreed with him, and said so.

"At least," Ferd said, sneaking a look at Niles, "the judge didn't get mad and take his anger out on Niles," he said.

''The judge was more sad than angry, I thought,'' Dan said. ''But you're right. Sometimes when life hands a person a bad backhand slap like the judge got today, they turn around and want to punish.''

He had to give the judge credit for that, at least.

He looked over to where Ferd was looking. Niles had been a lucky, lucky man.

He looked out the window at the livery stable across the street. The barn door was closed.

Then he saw Jay coming from up the still muddy street, carrying four tin cups of coffee on a tray from Big Alice's saloon.

''Niles,'' Dan said, ''would you mind staying an extra night, until we can come up with a solution on what to do? You can sleep on a cot, not in the cell,'' Dan said.

''Nah, I sleep in da cell,'' Niles said. ''I'm used to it,'' he added. ''Yust leave the door open to the cell.'' he said, agreeably.

''Do you want to go, right now? Leave town? Do you want the third thing, banishment?'' Ferd said, hopefully.

''Na,'' Niles said. ''I like it here. Nice pipples. Jay is nice pipple. Sheriff is nice pipple. Gimme da udder two tings. Jay, he's my friend. I like to stay. It's alright you giff me the lash. And da moneys ting. I work for you. I work it off.''

Ferd looked dubious at the very last thing. Let a robber work for him?

Jay came in with the coffee. Dan took a cup. It tasted good. If he wasn't mistaken, it had some whiskey in it. No one else mentioned it, as Niles, Ferd, Jay, and Dan sipped.

It was silent until Jay suddenly remembered something with a start. He pulled a letter out from where it was tucked in his trousers near his leather belt.

"This is for you, Dan. I think it's from Jeff. He left it at Alice's last night, to be delivered this morning. She just gave it to me." He handed him the letter. "Dan" was written across the front in the small, tight handwriting of Jeff Graywood. Inside it said:

> Sorry, Dan, to cause you all this trouble. It's not what you think. I'm just taking Jenny to the train. She is determined to go back East. She says that she is homesick for Philadelphia. That's where she came from. She begged me and begged me to take her to the train as soon as she realized that I was leaving, too. As for me, I don't want to spend the rest of my life in a livery stable. I need to try something new.
>
> People will say that she and I have run off to be together. You know me well enough to know that that is not the truth. Jenny will be on the Central Pacific train heading east by the time her husband finds out she is gone. I am sorry about the judge. He is a good man, and I am sorry that Jenny is going to hurt him, but it is unavoidable. If I didn't take her, she was planning to run off to Sacramento by herself and that is too dangerous.
>
> Please sell the livery stable for me, and send the money to the post office box that is listed below. The post office box belongs to my sister in San Francisco.
>
> Please hire someone to care for the livestock and run the livery stable until it can be sold. I have enclosed some money for that purpose, and the key to the stable door.
>
> Sorry.
>
> Your friend,
> Jeff Graywood

Below was a post office box number in San Francisco and the name Mrs. James O'Fallon. A key to the padlock on the stable door was included.

Dan put the letter, the money, and the key on his desk. Then he turned to Niles, Jay, and Ferd.

"A job just turned up, if it's all right with you, Ferd. Jay can show you how to do it, Niles."

Jay and Niles waited expectantly.

"This is a note from Jeff. I can hire you to care for the livestock over at the livery stable. That way, you can pay Ferd back whatever he agrees on."

Dan was not without doubts about this plan. But it had seemed to present itself as a temporary solution, at least, to a variety of problems. He'd have to watch carefully and allow it, one day at a time, until he saw how trustworthy Niles turned out to be.

Just to be certain, he'd let Jay take care of all the money at the livery stable, for now. It would be good, common sense to downplay Niles's role at the stable, have it just be known as part of Niles's punishment—which in effect it was—to work off his debt to Ferd.

It was important not to appear to reward Niles in any way for what he had done. There was Dennis, for one, to think of. He was watching to see what would happen to Niles.

He decided to come down hard on Niles, just so that there would be no misunderstanding.

"I'll be watching you closer than any chicken hawk ever watched a chicken, Turgstrom," he said.

"Oh, I know, I know," Niles said, moving away from Dan and closer to Jay.

"I troo wit da life of crimes," Niles said.

"You better be," Dan said. "I'm trusting you here. Giving you a second chance. So is Ferd, here. He is the one who has the most to lose, besides yourself, if you mess up. There'll be no more chances."

Niles looked scared to death.

"You want I should start right now, acrost the street?" Niles asked, looking at both Ferd and Dan.

Ferd answered, seemingly glad to get rid of the man. "I do," Ferd said.

Dan took the key off the desk and handed it to Jay.

"I'll be only too glad to show you how to do a job that I had for a long time," Jay said, patting Niles on the shoulder as he opened the door for them to leave. "It's called mucking out the stalls," he added as the door closed behind the two men. Jay turned to look in a joking manner back at Dan.

Dan sighed.

He'd miss Jeff. A lot. He was a man that had a lot of common sense, good character, and the ability to doctor sick horses and mules beyond what Dan had ever seen any other man able to do. He wondered if Jeff had made the right decision today. He hoped Jeff would be happy. Life was full of decisions that once made, were hard to undo.

Ferd stood waiting until he saw, through the window, that Jay had opened the stable door, and that he and Niles had gone inside.

"Another twenty-three dollars and forty-seven cents will do it," Ferd said, finally, thinking. "That would make it double."

"No. I think the judge meant not including the original twenty-three dollars and forty-seven cents stolen," Dan said. "That would be forty-six dollars and ninety four cents. That would be double. You can't count the original stolen money as part of the double,'' Dan said.

''You want to come and work as my bookkeeper?'' Ferd said. ''That's pretty smart thinking.''

''I don't want to make it too easy on Niles,'' Dan said. ''I have my own reasons,'' he said, thinking of Dennis.

''What about the stripes?'' Ferd said.

''I'll let you take care of that part of it, if you don't mind,'' Dan said. ''I may be sheriff, and I'll kill if I have to, but I don't have much of a stomach for whipping. But if you don't mind,'' he said to the kind-hearted Ferd, ''I'd consider it a favor if you'd keep that information to yourself.''

''Consider it done.'' Ferd said. ''Maybe only ten lashes. I'll have to *hire* someone to do it. I feel the same way as you do about it.''

''Maybe Jay,'' Dan said, grinning. ''Maybe Jay would do it.''

Ferd chuckled.

''Doubt it. Don't know who we could find. Mebbe the judge,'' he said, chuckling. ''Nah. He won't do it, neither,'' he added, once he thought it over.

Chapter Nineteen

Before dawn, on Thursday, Jay drove up in front of Dan's house in a wagon with three barrels inside the wagon bed. Alister and Dan were already up, and had eaten breakfast by the time they heard the rattle of the wagon arriving. Jay and Dan lugged out the bags of gold to the front porch, and then into the wagon bed. Then Alister, Dan, and Jay climbed into the wagon and began to hide the gold in the barrels.

The three men agreed as they worked, that Alister and Jay would carry only the guns that they did regularly, there was no sense looking liked armed guards and alerting the suspicions of people who might be aware of things like that.

"In Texas, I used to carry my bit of money tied up in my shirttail," Alister said, as he was banging the lid tightly back on one of the barrels.

Just as dawn was breaking, the two men drove off, and Dan blew out the oil lamp that they had been working by. He went back into the dim house. They might be gone two or three days, by the time Alister completed all his business in Red Bluff.

By nine-thirty, Dan had checked with both judges. The case against King was moving along rapidly. Everyone would feel sorry for his wife and family, when the news broke, Dan knew. They would have to deal with the coming disgrace, loss of money, home, and everything else when the law moved against Harvey to get the victims' money back. Dan hoped that Dennis would get back some of the money that was his, as well as K. G. James and others.

Nights, when he was not busy with keeping order in the saloons, Dan was out near Black's chicken farm, keeping an eye out for chicken thieves while patrolling the woods behind the coop.

Alister came back and set up a new bank in the vacant general store. He was having a large green and white sign painted that said Forest Grove Cheap Bank. Dan had tried to persuade him to leave off the word cheap but Alister had insisted.

Dan was busy, and at first, he paid almost no attention to the school contest.

Days, Dan was busy watching that Niles was working out across the street in the livery stable. He seemed to be doing all right there, but Dan couldn't shake off an uneasy feeling. Niles was living up over the stable now.

It was a while before he noticed that Dennis, who was one of Horace's students, was coming to church, and slipping into the pew beside Dan as usual and chewing on his fingernails, biting them down to the quick and making them bleed.

Outside, Dan asked Dennis what was the matter. First he asked him if everything was all right at the pastor's house.

"Fine, they're real nice," Dennis said. "They let me go over to Mrs. Nedlinger's house to tend the goats when my homework's done."

Then Dan asked, "How's school?"

Dennis's expression changed. It was as if a dark cloud passed over his face.

"Okay," he said.

"I see you have been biting your nails," Dan said.

"Oh, it's that dang test," Dennis said. "Been doin' a lot of studyin'. Thoughts of that dang test make me nervous. Mr. Blackthorn says we *have* to win." He added, "The pastor has been helping me study at night."

"I see," Dan said.

"How are you and Mrs. Nedlinger getting along?"

Dennis grinned.

"Just fine. She's putting my earnings aside. Says I can have that baby goat soon. It's coming from Red Bluff." Dennis returned to Mrs. Cook's side and they walked off toward the pastor's house.

It was the pastor who approached Dan, after the contest was over. He showed up at Dan's house on a Saturday morning. The test had been taken on Friday.

Alister had moved out and was living in a back room of his new bank. Little did Alister know, that shortly, his might be the only bank in town.

"Come in, Pastor Cook," Dan said. He had just completed his chores, and was surprised to see the pastor at his house so early.

''Is Dennis all right?'' Dan asked.

''What? Oh, yes,'' Pastor Cook said, ''Oh, I guess you're relieved that I didn't come about Dennis. Well, in an odd way, I guess I did.''

Pastor Cook took the pile of papers he had in his hand and spread them out so Dan could see them, carefully not putting them near Dan's tin cup that was full of hot, dark, strong coffee.

''You want some coffee, or some breakfast?'' Dan asked.

''No, no.'' the pastor said. ''Please look at these tests, here.''

Dan looked.

''What about them?'' He looked. The tests were questions about Greek mythology.

''Look, here, look. 'Who is King of Mount Olympus?' The answer is Zeus. 'Whose bow could shoot arrows of flame and pestilence?' The answer is Apollo. 'Who was the goddess of beauty?' Over here, Venus. These are the tests from Horace's class.''

''I can see that.'' He looked at the names of the students that were on the top of the pages. He knew which students attended Horace's schoolroom and which students attended Cassie's.

''Here, look more closely. Do you notice anything?''

Dan studied. Then he realized what it was that the pastor was pointing out.

Three original—wrong—answers had been scratched out and the correct answers written in over the scratched-out ones. In a grown-up's handwriting . . . one that Dan recognized very well. It was Horace's handwriting.

Horace had clearly changed answers to make his students

win the contest. It appeared that Dennis had not one incorrect answer, but at least four had been scratched out and changed.

"I haven't totaled the grades, yet. I came here, first. What will I do?" Pastor Cook said. "The test should be taken over! What can I do?"

Dan knew that he was saying that to accuse Horace directly would just result in a denial difficult or impossible to disprove.

"It's too bad that that coffee is right near my elbow. It looks like it might tip over," Pastor Cook said. "That is, if I'm not careful when I move my elbow here. Might not be able to complete grading those papers, with all those coffee stains. And the result might be that the test would have to be taken over, in front of witnesses, and with you and I grading them without the teachers getting their hands on them first."

The parson looked shocked at himself, at his own idea. The idea that had just come to him.

Dan didn't answer.

He was thinking it over. Horace had been crooked, was a poor teacher, and a general pain in the arse.

Dan didn't come to a decision. It was a dilemma. He was still thinking.

But Pastor Cook did. Slowly, with much thought, his elbow slowly jutted out a bit, knocking Dan's coffee cup over.

Dan was shocked.

"Oh, Sheriff, I'm so sorry," the pastor said. "And look what a terrible thing I've done. I've spoiled the papers. The test will have to be repeated Monday, first thing. And I, myself, shall see to it that God's will, will be done. *Fairly.* Amen.''

With that, he gathered up the ''spoiled'' papers, and bowed his head and said devoutly, ''Lord, forgive us our trespasses. Amen.''

To Dan, he said, sorrowfully, ''The lesser of two evils. Spilled coffee or let Horace get away with this. I accept total responsibility for what I have done.''

He looked at Dan, as he always had, with respect.

''When the results of the new tests are in, whether they are drastically different or not, I will tell the community of my sin and let them decide if they still want me, a lying sinner, for their pastor. I will abide by the results of their decision. But for the time being, this is the only practical solution I can come up with.''

Without saying anything further, he left.

Early Monday morning, as good as his word, he appeared unexpectedly at Horace's school with the same test to be retaken.

Dan appeared at Cassie's with the same thing.

Horace took a fit, but when Dan and Pastor Cook corrected the new tests, the ''cat was out of the bag.'' Horace disappeared after school that very day, before the tests were even corrected. His clothing and possessions were gone, cleaned out of the bedroom in the Zachary's home. The Zachary children cheered as he went out of sight down the road.

Dennis got a seventy-four on his test.

The pastor made good on his word and told the congregation on the next Sunday what he had done. To a person, they voted for him to stay.

All the students were transferred to Cassie's school.

Chapter Twenty

The second chance for Niles was not to be, Dan found out. Before the whipping could be scheduled, when only eight dollars of the forty-six dollars and ninety-four cents had been paid, Niles was dead.

Three men arrived in town an hour before nightfall and boldly attempted to rob the livery stable, across from the sheriff's office. There was no money there. It was across the street in Dan's office, locked in a desk drawer for safe-keeping. When Niles protested that there wasn't any money, the robbers thought he was lying and shot him, Niles said before he died.

Jay heard shots, and ran across the street and saw the three robbers jump on their horses and hightail it back out of town. Niles died in Jay's arms shortly after he had told his story of what happened.

Dan was out visiting his father's and mother's graves

when it happened. It was the first time he'd had a chance to do it since his mother had been laid to rest.

Jay had gotten a good look at the robbers. He'd been watching as they rode in and dismounted in front of the stable. Rough-looking men were not an unusual occurrence in town, so Jay didn't pay too close attention until he heard shots.

After covering Niles's dead body in the livery stable with a clean horse blanket, Jay ran to tell the undertaker, and then to try to gather men for a posse.

Dan, riding back into town shortly after the killing, saw the commotion at the stable, found out what had happened, and then hurried across the street to his office, where he hurriedly gathered what he needed: another pistol, his rifle, ammunition, some rope, and some small sheets of paper as well as the new steel pen that his mother had gotten him as a present for Christmas. It had come all the way from Camden, New Jersey.

Mrs. Nedlinger, who obviously hadn't heard the news yet, walked in the door of his office just as he was about to leave. She evidently had ignored the ruckus across the street, intent on her business with Dan.

"Been thinking," she began abruptly as she walked in. "Think I will take Dennis, after all. Been workin' out fine, so far, me an' him."

"That's great news," Dan said. Not wanting to hurry her, but thinking that she couldn't have come at a worse time; he had to get going. He had to get home and get supplies. He was leaving right away and Jay and whoever he could get would follow his tracks as soon as they could.

The tracking shouldn't be too hard, the earth was still

muddy enough so that a hoof would sink down an inch or two.

"I talked to Pastor Cook and he said he would bring him over, but I thought it would be better if I went and got Dennis."

"Good." Dan said. "You've made me a happy man, Nellie."

The killers had a thirty minute start on Dan.

"I have to go. Sorry to rush you," he said, "But there's been a killing."

"Oh, my, no," Mrs. Nedlinger said, following him out the door.

He locked it.

"Real happy about your decision," he said, swinging up on Sarah and sticking his rifle in the sheath as he spoke.

Mrs. Nedlinger nodded, and then really noticing for the first time the crowd across the street in the stable, she turned and went over there.

Using his reins, Dan turned Sarah and directed the horse on up the street where, once again, he stopped at his own home to load up on food. He swung the small canvas sack of food up and hung it from his saddle, and tied his bedroll on behind him. There was no telling how long he'd be gone.

In another minute Dan was on his way toward the mountains, following the tracks of three men. From Jay's description, these were not flatlanders, or Easterners. To Jay they looked like men who were tough, and familiar with mountain survival.

Dan tracked the men. He hoped that something had caused them to stop, so that he wasn't too far behind.

Because there were three, he'd have to try to wing one

or two to even the odds. If he was able, by shortcuts, to come upon them, he'd circle around them and try to do just that.

Dusk was only a half hour away; Dan easily followed the tracks in the mud leading east. It looked like they were foolish enough—or experienced enough—to try to go up the mountain the locals called the Big Y.

He came to a spot where the killers had dismounted and walked over a large area of flat gray boulders buried in the ground, to try to make whoever followed them lose the trail. It took a while, circling around, for Dan to pick up their trail where they had left the boulder area. Pine needles made his search more difficult.

When he found it, he stuck the thin strip of bright red cloth (already tied to the top of a short stick) that he took out of his saddlebag into the ground as a marker so that the posse didn't have to waste the same amount of time looking but could follow right along.

Jay and Dan had what they jokingly called a ''strip and stick'' system. Some of the red strips of cloth were tied to a stick, and it took Dan—when he was tracking someone and a posse was to follow him—only seconds to dismount and to jam a stick with the red cloth already tied to it, in the ground for Jay to use to follow Dan's trail. Other strips of red cloth in his saddlebag didn't have sticks attached, they were for tying directly to a bough of a pine tree wherever that was a better choice or more obvious to a following tracker or posse.

The trouble was, it already was getting dark.

Fast.

The posse wouldn't be able to see the red cloth until daylight.

Dan followed the trail as long as there was the slightest light. Once, he stopped to let Sarah take a drink in a swift-moving, bubbling stream. Then he made camp, just off the trail to the right, on a level spot surrounded by pines. As he fed Sarah some barley he had brought, he kept alert for any smell of smoke. There was none, so far as he could tell.

He didn't make a fire, either.

No coffee.

Dang. He would have liked some.

He took a drink from his canteen.

The posse, even if it was not far behind him, would not be reaching him tonight. It would be a long night. He pulled some jerky out of the canvas bag, and picketed Sarah for the night.

Then he unrolled his blanket and got in.

He breathed deeply, ready to go to sleep.

Wood smoke!

A faint smell of woodsmoke nearby!

He'd like to move Sarah away in case she made a noise—especially an answering whinny if she heard another horse nearby—but the trouble was, he didn't know in which direction to move her. And she might make noise moving. The weight of her feet were enough to make a loud clop, clop noise in the dead silence around him.

In the dark, he moved close to her and spoke to her in a whisper.

"Quiet girl, those are not our friends," he whispered. Then he froze, trying to locate which direction the smell was coming from.

For once, there was hardly any wind. No breeze making

soft noises in the pines to muffle any noise he made in the dark like stepping on a twig and snapping it.

Finally, he detected a very slight breeze.

Tense, he slid his feet in the direction of the slight breeze, upwind, hoping it wasn't one of those breezes that fool you by circling around a bit instead of coming straight on. Sometimes the ravines tended to play tricks with the wind.

Leaving Sarah where she was, his gun loosened and ready, he crept slowly, sliding his feet more than picking them up and putting them down, hoping that that way he could avoid snapping dead pine twigs or boughs that had broken off in a recent wind.

It was the almost blue-black of early nightfall. He could see mostly the black profiles of where things were rather than where they weren't.

He reached the top of a ravine, feeling his way slowly and cautiously in the dark, all the time mapping in his mind the route back to Sarah—telling himself never mind the blanket in case of a necessary quick getaway, a skedaddle. He came to the edge of the ravine.

Very, very slowly he lowered himself to the ground, then finally lying all the way down flat he could hear a conversation below him. He took off his hat and raised his head just the smallest bit over the edge and looked down.

From the voices, it was a unique, shallow ravine, because unless they were talking loudly—which he believed they weren't—they were probably only twenty feet below him.

Smart, they had made a very small campfire directly under one of the pine trees, so that the smoke would dissipate up through the pine needles and not make a noticeable white or gray trail upward. The light from the fire was so faint he couldn't make out any distinct shapes. The irony was that they were so close—probably due to Dan's short-cuts—that it was the faint smell itself that Dan had recognized.

It was a smell he liked.

"Gimme some more a that brown gargle," Dan heard a voice say.

He heard the clank of a tin cup bump up against an enamel coffee pot; it was a sound he was well familiar with.

There was a grunt, indicating thanks.

"I still say we shot the wrong man," a gruff, unfriendly, take-no-nonsense voice said. He sounded like a third man, not one of the two asking for, or pouring the coffee.

The voice came a little from the left of the other two voices, and sounded authoritarian, like the voice of a leader not a follower. And not like the voice of a man who particularly cared if they had shot the wrong man. It had a quality of not caring except it might mean that they'd have to try again.

"It's him, I tell you. We got Alister Skinner," the first voice said.

Alister!

Chapter Twenty-one

They were arguing over whether they had shot Alister!

The voice of the leader spoke again.

"Something about him . . . he didn't fit the description that King gave us. Harvey didn't mention nothin' about no foreign accent. That guy had an accent—German or something."

He didn't seem to know the difference between a German accent and a Scandinavian accent.

"Anyways, Skinner ain't a German name," the leader continued.

"That don't mean nothin'. Maybe his mother was German," the voice of the man who asked for coffee said.

"Shut up, you dang fool," said a voice from where the coffee-pourer sat. "Listen to him. I think he's right. What are we going to do now, if he's right? King ain't gonna pay us for no job that ain't been done."

"Don't worry about it. We been workin' for him so long, he won't mind one mix up. He won't care if no German got kilt by mistake, as long's we git the right man next time," the leader's voice said.

"Did we git any money? So that they'll say it was a robbery like we planned?" He took a loud slurp of his coffee.

"No, you stupid fool. Can't you remember, even, what happened just a few hours ago? You were there, stupid. Remember that the guy didn't have but fifty-seven cents or so on him. Jeez, you're stupid. That's why you shot him before we could find out his name for sure," the coffee-pourer said.

"Oh, yeah," the voice said vaguely. "Now I remember."

"What do you bother with him for, Mr. O.? He's so dang ingnorant that he can't remember where he was this afternoon!" the coffee pourer said.

"He has his good points," the leader said. "When I say point that .44 and shoot, you can't find no better than Rufus, here. Right Rufus?"

"Right. I point and shoot real good."

"He don't ask no million stupid questions neither," the leader's voice continued. There was an ominous threat in his voice.

The thought ran through Dan's mind that he was saying that he could tell Rufus right now to shoot the talker—the coffee pourer—and that Rufus would. Instantly and without regret.

There was silence.

"I'm turning in," the threatened man said, eager to change the talk to something less dangerous.

''No, wait,'' the leader said. ''I think there's something out there.''

Dan froze.

He was sure that he had made no sound. He had not moved even the smallest muscle. Yet the man down there sensed something.

''Go on out there a take a look,'' the leader said to the man he had just threatened.

''Me?'' the man asked.

''You!'' he said, leaving no doubt that if he wasn't directly obeyed, there would be consequences that the man could only too well imagine.

''And check up there, above us, on the ridge,'' the leader said.

''Now,'' the leader commanded through clenched teeth.

The man—the coffee pourer—appeared frightened of going out in the woods by himself. Reluctantly, he crept away from the fire and went to the right, walking along the bottom of the ravine. He was probably looking for a spot to climb up. The slope directly below Dan was too steep either to go up or down.

Dan had only a split second to decide whether to speak out now, or to try to divide and conquer.

He had the advantage on the man disappearing in the ravine in that he knew what was happening and the man didn't know for certain if there was even anyone there, or where Dan was. Evidently, he had no sixth sense like the leader down below seemed to have.

The leader had made a mistake. Dan would have had trouble facing down three at once, alone. But one . . . and one who seemed to be frightened of the dark, at that.

The thing was to get out of hearing range of the two

down below without being detected, and to take care of the lone man, the coffee pourer, wandering at night in the dark woods.

The man might come upon Sarah.

Dan hoped that luck would be with him, not with the man searching for him.

Using his arm muscles only, he very slowly raised up the upper part of his body, and then when that was raised, he carefully bent his knees forward so that he was squatting, and then he raised himself up silently.

Down below, he heard the leader say, ''When he comes back, Rufus, kill him.''

''Yep,'' Rufus said, his voice not indicating the slightest regret.

''Asked too many questions,'' the leader said in explanation.

Dan knelt back down and felt for his hat, then crept back from the edge of the ravine—out of sight—and put his hat back on. He crept back, a little at a time, until he was, he hoped, safely out of hearing of the two men below. Then as silently as possible he moved back through the dark shadowy woods to where he calculated that he might cross the path of the man sent to hunt him.

The moon, pale at first, was growing brighter as it rose above the horizon.

He walked slowly back a short distance from the top edge of the ravine until he came to a place where the man would likely choose to come up, as it was a place that seemed less steep than where he had lain and listened.

He waited behind one of the thick very tall pines until he heard very, very soft footsteps, and then he ever so slowly withdrew his pistol from its holster and turned it so the butt end was forward. He waited, breathing only very shallowly, as the man came up the ravine and slowly walked closer and closer up the ridge toward him. Finally, when Dan could stand the waiting and suspense no longer, he stepped out and brought his pistol butt down as hard as he could on the top of the man's head.

The man slid to the ground with a soft groan.

Dan bent down, squatted, and slung the unconscious man over his shoulder, and then, keeping his back straight, he stood back up.

In the dark, Dan could feel that the man was a scrawny one who had never done any physical labor, at least not for a long time. He weighed only about a hundred and forty pounds, if that, Dan said to himself as he held onto the man quietly lying over his shoulder. Dan carried him back to where he'd left Sarah and his blanket.

He took the man's gun and tied the man up securely, and then he untied the blue handkerchief that he had put around his own neck that morning and tied it tightly around the mouth of the man, effectively gagging him.

Dan thought for a second, and then grabbed his blanket and threw it up, folded loosely, on the horse. Then he flung the still unconscious man over Sarah's saddle, and set out.

The map of the day's ride still in his head, Dan walked Sarah, with the man flung over her, back to the last strip and stick that he had left.

When he reached the place where he had left it, Dan pulled the man down off the horse and searched him for knives and other things that the outlaw might use to untie himself. Clearing the area of sharp rocks as best he could in the semidarkness, he tied the man to the tree in the center of where he had cleared.

The man was recovering consciousness, so Dan spoke to him.

"This is the Sheriff. Don't bother trying to go back to Mr. O. and Rufus. They were planning to shoot you when you returned to the campfire."

There was no response from the man and Dan didn't know if he even heard Dan's advice.

He had done him a favor in even mentioning it as the man would have saved Dan some trouble if he returned to them and was shot. One less outlaw to worry about.

Dan left the man securely tied to the tree, then laid the blanket over him. If things went well, shortly after dawn, the posse would come upon the outlaw very near the marker. What had happened would be clear to Jay.

Dan still didn't know the man's name. He thought of him only as the coffee pourer.

His mind was racing as he quietly snuck back near where he was camped before. He would move to a different spot, just in case, but he was thinking as he went: Rufus and the other man were the real killers.

Rufus had seemed to Dan to be one of those men who was able to kill without comprehending what he had done: to send a man to the hereafter without even a blink's worth of second thoughts.

Is a man born that way, or is there something that he isn't taught by his parents?

"There's right and there's wrong," his own father and mother used to say. "You do one or the other. If you do 'the other,' you must bear the consequences. You might still be walking around alive," his father used to say, "but you *might as well be dead.* For you have no pride in yerself. Ain't added nothin' good to the world to prove that the fact that you been livin's a good thing.''

What to do next?

Go back to the campfire and confront Rufus and Mr. O.? Or wait until dawn?

Maybe go now, while he had the element of darkness and surprise on his side.

When he got back to the place where the two men had been, they appeared to be gone.

He waited above the ravine where the abandoned campfire was, to see if it was a trap.

Nothing. It was quiet, no unusual noises in the night.

Evidently when the coffee pourer had not returned, the leader had decided that leaving was a smart idea.

After waiting a while, Dan crept down to the abandoned campfire and held his hand over the ashes to see how hot they were. Pretty cool. Evidently they had been gone since shortly after the coffee pourer had left the campfire.

There was no chance of tracking them until first light. Dan took Sarah and moved off about a quarter of a mile and lay down, using his hat as a pillow, somewhat regretting his kindness to the coffee pourer, as it left him to bear the cold of the night with nothing but the clothes he had on his back.

During the day the sun made the temperature hot enough here to give you a bad sunburn if you went hatless but at night the heavy dew and the rapid drop in temperature sometimes made two blankets a necessity, sometimes even inside a house or cabin.

It was a two blanket night.

His stomach rumbled.

The thought of the jerky, so far his only supper, made

Dan remember what someone had told him once. In the Northeast, meat rotted if left out in the open air.

Here in the West, it practically made life possible in that it dried out in the sun, it didn't rot. It must be odd to have meat rot like that.

He got out some hardtack and chewed it.

He didn't dare break off pine boughs to make a bed. The snapping of the bough branches might attract the murderers.

Too cold to really sleep, he just waited out the night until he finally dozed off toward morning.

Chapter Twenty-two

At first light, still tired from lack of sleep, he rose and made his way back to where the campfire had been. There, he found his way back down into the ravine and picked up the trail, once again happy in his good luck that the ground was still damp—something that during the long nighttime hours he had cursed plenty.

He would have used Sarah's saddle blanket, but he had left Sarah saddled as a precaution in case the robbers returned and stalked him in the night. It was something he didn't like to do.

He gave Sarah a handful of barley from the small bag inside his saddlebag before he swung back up on her. A drink would have to wait for the first stream they came to.

He mounted and then they set off again.

Once he got down and checked the tracks in the damp earth. Crusted, they had begun to dry out and crumble back into the hoofprints. Not a good sign. They had a good start on him once again.

The trail went through some narrow places, places that if it had been raining would have been treacherous. The sun had not yet come out; instead there was a cold fog. Steep hillsides surrounded him on both sides as Sarah made her way carefully along the narrow trail.

Dan thought some on "the leader," as he called him in his head. This man was not stupid, nor a fool. He wondered about the man's behavior last night.

Mr. O.

Dan didn't really believe in a sixth sense but he did believe that some people have either above average hearing, or sense of smell or sight—or all of these things—that they pick up on things that most people would miss.

Had he heard Dan's breathing?

Dan had heard stories about an Indian woman who knew when the cavalry was near and had saved her brother, a warrior, more than once by this ability.

Red rock ledges and gravel appeared on both sides of the trail. Something surprising was happening. Dan realized that the two men he was tracking were heading downward, off the Big Y.

The sun came out and the mist burned off.

It began to get hot.

Hour after hour Dan followed the trail, winding downward and northeast. Once the grade was so steep that he got down off Sarah and walked, so that he didn't get pitched off forward over her ears.

Dan hoped that they weren't heading toward where, more and more, he thought they were going. A place where there was an abandoned cabin.

A place he hated to go.

A place that he had been putting off going to even though an educated woman had given him sound solid advice, which he hadn't taken. To put a sign there.

Rattlesnake Gulch.

Suddenly, on a small granite rock in the path, Sarah stumbled.

Dang!

Quickly, he got down and examined her leg. It didn't look serious but Sarah's ankle was scraped and bloody. He felt her ankle gently. No bones broken. Nothing twisted beyond repair. But he couldn't ride her and cause more damage. He'd have to go on and leave her for Jay and the posse to look after her.

Dan left a red marker, and picketed Sarah in sight of the trail. He left Jay the bag of barley, and a quick, scribbled note in the saddlebag. He said that he thought that the men were on their way to Rattlesnake Gulch, and to take care of Sarah.

Now on foot, with his guns, rifle, ammunition, canteen, knife, and the bag of food, Dan set out.

The two men ahead had three horses. They had the coffee-pourer's horse with them. They could change-off riding and give one horse at a time a rest.

Night fell, and it was another miserable night spent, this time, without even Sarah to keep him company.

He realized that he hadn't eaten very much all day and he pulled some beef jerky out of the bag and ate it with some hardtack. He chewed the hard, coarse bread, grateful to have it.

In the army, he had been issued hardtack more than once, only to find it full of pieces of dead, crushed insects, baked right in—either ants or cockroaches, he didn't know which. He'd had to throw it away in disgust.

It was about four o'clock the next afternoon when he arrived at the area that was familiar to him. He came upon it from the southeast, rather than from the southwest, so he was up away from the crest of the ridge he'd ridden to with Sarah. He worked his way down so that he came to the cabin cautiously, keeping behind the ridge facing it. He took off his hat and laid down and peered over the ridge, and looked down at the cabin.

The three horses were not in sight.

It looked quiet down there, but smoke was coming out of the chimney. He would make an easy target if he went directly down the slope of the gulch to the cabin.

A plan came to him.

He eased back from the ridge out of sight, put his hat back on, and then followed the ridge down for about a quarter of a mile past the cabin. Sighting a place where he could get down the slope to the stream, he checked his pistol, making sure it was loosened in his holster, checked his rifle, and made sure that it was loaded. He looked cautiously around, and then dropped the food bag.

He was ready.

He went down the slope, crossed the stream which miraculously was still low, and, on the side of the stream that the cabin was on, crept along the steep back of the gulch until he came to the grove of scraggly cottonwoods in back of the cabin. Not much to his surprise, the three horses were hidden in the cottonwoods.

He quietly untied and led them, one at a time, back downstream where he had come from, and retied them out of sight in a clearing in a clump of pines he had noticed on his way upstream.

Then he went back to the clump of cottonwoods behind the cabin.

What should he do?

Should he call out, or attempt to sneak up on the cabin? Or should he wait until one of the men came out, and try to take them one at a time?

Or should he just wait for the posse? They ought to have caught up by now—he was walking and they were riding, so they ought to have been here by now—but obviously they weren't. Had deciding what to do about Sarah caused some slowdown, some arguments?

He trusted Jay. Jay knew how Dan felt about Sarah.

As if to decide his argument, the door of the cabin opened, and Rufus came out. Dan lowered his rifle to the ground, and eased his U.S. army Colt .44 out of the holster with his left hand. More than once, a gunman had been surprised to see that Dan was a left-handed shooter.

Oddly, Rufus looked different in the daylight than Dan expected.

Something was wrong.

Dan didn't have time to stop and figure it out, but something had happened to Rufus's vicious attitude. He was looking worried as he left the doorway of the cabin without looking around first, something that Dan judged to be a less than smart thing to do. Rufus hurriedly walked down to the stream's edge with a bucket. Lowering it and swirling it as it filled, he pulled it back up out of the water and turned, just as Dan reached the corner of the cabin—out of the gunshot line of the doorway and the single window which was glassless and covered only with half-rotten canvas on the inside. It was on the front side of the house facing the stream.

There were no windows on the side of the shack facing Dan, although there was no guarantee that the other man—the leader, Mr. O—was actually inside and not creeping up behind to shoot Dan in the back.

As Rufus turned with the bucket of water, he saw that Dan had the drop on him.

It happened so quickly, Dan had no choice. No time to talk.

Rufus dropped the bucket and drew his gun so fast that Dan only had a split second to prepare himself for what was coming next.

They shot at the same time, Dan aiming as best he could at the gun arm of the man.

He had some protection in that he was close to the shack. Rufus was out in the open.

Rufus fell as a bullet flew by Dan's head.

Dan turned, expecting to see the leader's gun appear out of the cabin door.

It seemed like minutes, but it was really only seconds as Dan realized that there had been no response from Mr. O. inside the shack.

It could be, very possibly, a trap.

Dan waited, and then he inched his way slowly to the cabin door. This time, he was the target out in the open.

With the barrel of his revolver going around the corner first, he slowly and cautiously, moved his head forward so that he could peer inside the cabin door.

Inside, lying half off the bed in the corner was Mr. O.

"You got Rufus," Mr. O. said. It was a statement, not

a question. ''Come in, then.'' he continued. ''No use me killin' you when you're the only hope I got.''

Dan looked around the small cabin. There was no one else inside but the huge hulk of Mr. O. sprawled there.

As he stepped inside, Dan saw part of what had happened.

''Snake in my boot,'' was all the man said.

Chapter Twenty-three

It made a clear enough picture for Dan to piece together what had happened. There was a boot, a dirty sock, and a dead snake in front of the bed, and the bottom part of the man's trousers were torn open to show where he and Rufus had tried to care for the wound on the man's right foot.

The man had no reason to suspect that if he left his boot lying down, a snake might crawl into it during the night. If his boot had been stood up, the snake might not have gotten in there.

An empty cabin attracts mice and other creatures, and a snake goes where prey is likely to be. A night hunter, in the early morning hours the snake had probably looked for something convenient to hole up in for the coming day. He'd found a boot.

A bloody knife on the bed next to the man, along with

some bloody rags, showed how he and Rufus had tried to get the poison out of the bite.

Mr. O. reached over and threw the knife on the floor to indicate that he was not going to try to use it on Dan.

"Hand me your pistol, butt first, and I'll see what I can do," Dan said.

"My brother—"

"Rufus was your brother?"

Mr. O. nodded.

Accepting the pistol, Dan took a look at the wound. Two good-sized puncture wounds were in the worst place possible—right on the man's big toe.

The man knew it. Already the toe and foot were huge with swelling, and badly discolored.

"Looks bad, don't it?"

"I'm not going to lie to you," Dan said. "Foot and toe wounds are among the worst."

He went outside the cabin and filled the bucket that had been dropped by Rufus and returned to the cabin.

He took a rag and began washing out the puncture wounds as best he could.

They had already been cut open to try to bleed the poison out, probably by Rufus, he saw.

Abruptly, as he cleaned the blood off so that he could see better, Dan asked "Harvey King hire you?"

The man nodded, yes.

Dan guessed that the poison had had a long time to circulate—it looked bad. The man was obviously in pain.

"Worked for him a lot of years, off and on, when he needed us. Supposed to kill a man named Alister Skinner. Knew too much. Did we get 'im?"

"No. Shot another man."

"Thought so. My brother, he ain't never been too bright. I allus had to take care of him. Had a short fuse. Never could figger things out straight."

He grimaced in pain.

"Meet my Maker soon. Done some bad things. Didn't regret none of it at the time, but now . . ." he grimaced again.

Things were going to get worse, and they both knew it.

"Gimme some of that whiskey?" the man said. He pointed, with great effort, to a small flask on the table.

"Not a good idea. Speeds up the poison's circulation. Had some experience with snakebit people," Dan said, giving him fair warning.

"What's the difference anyway? I'm done for. Look at the size of that snake."

Dan agreed with the man's assessment of the situation, but didn't say so. He gave him the flask.

He heard the sound of horses and riders outside.

"Dan, you in there?" Jay called anxiously, as if from a distance.

"Yes. Come on in."

Dan finished cleaning the wound as best he could.

"You don't owe me nothin'," the man said, "but I'm gonna ask you a favor anyways, Sheriff."

"What is it?" Dan said, noticing that the man's color was already changing to an odd gray-greenish, almost purple.

As Jay's footsteps reached the door and he entered, the man said, "Bury me next to Rufus, will ya? I'd kind of like to still take care of him in the Great Beyond."

Dan nodded to Jay as he entered, and then said, "I think

I can do that much. Especially if you tell my deputy here, what you just told me about Harvey King.''

Crooked Charlie stuck his head in the door. Jay and Dan motioned for him to come in and Crooked Charlie listened as the man told of what he had done over the years for Harvey King. Five other members of the posse crowded into the room to hear the man's confession, also. It was enough to cook Harvey King's goose and then some. A dying man's confession was held as sacred truth.

About five in the afternoon, the posse buried the two men, Rufus and Cyrus Overbrook—Mr. O. was short for Overbrook—on the ridge on the opposite side of the stream, overlooking Rattlesnake Gulch.

The third man, the coffee pourer, was with the posse and would be brought back to town to face Judge Herbert. His name was George Nash.

Sarah was being walked slowly back to Dan's barn by Ferd Cody.

On the way back to River Grove, Crooked Charlie rode alongside Dan.

''I got a question to ask.''

''Ask away.''

''It is true that you are the person to see to purchase the livery stable?''

''Why, you interested?''

''Yes.'' Crooked Charlie said in his soft accent.

''Mind if I ask why?''

Crooked Charlie looked embarrassed.

''I'm thinking of closing the saloon. Taking the sign down. Think I'm through with all that. Time for me, maybe, to get respectable.''

Dan looked over to see if Charlie was joking. He looked perfectly serious.

"Fact is," he continued, "I kind of got my eye on Julia Anderson. She's a lady. A real lady. I figure that if I got myself all respectable . . ."

He shifted his body uneasily in the saddle and said, "Fact is, I been to her house to see her a few times lately. Seems she'd consent to have me if I give up gamblin' and such."

Dan guessed that the "and such" meant the saloon.

"You think you could?"

"I think I could. I think it's time I give up bein' so bitter about the war and begin livin' a *real* life again. What's past is past, Julia's been tellin' me. An' I think maybe she's right. I been watchin' Julia with Moira and I think she'd make a real fine mother."

"I have to agree with that."

"I'll be in your office next Monday morning to discuss the price then," Crooked Charlie said.

"I'll be looking forward to it," Dan said.

Crooked Charlie dropped back to stay with Jay when Jay stopped to give his horse a rest. Jay was riding double, with the prisoner, George Nash, on the back of his horse.

Back in town, Dan picked up Harvey King at the bank and shortly after that, Harvey King, protesting vigorously, occupied one cell.

George Nash occupied the other as soon as Jay arrived.

Alister was more than a slightly happy man.

In fact, Dan heard him walking up the street singing "Comin' Through the Rye."

Dan went home. He was hungry, dirty, and tired.

He walked into the barn, first, to care for Sarah. Ferd

had done a good job bringing her home. The scratch near her hoof was clean and cared for and looked like it was going to be all right.

Sarah would be fine.

Dan would have to ride another horse for the next few days, though.

He walked past the empty chicken coops, glad that he no longer had to deal with chickens as part of his everyday chores. It reminded him that he had one more thing still hanging over his head.

He had solved all the major problems but one. And that he would take care of as soon as he had eaten, bathed, and slept.

He went in the house and made supper, took a bath, and then fell into bed, exhausted.

Chapter Twenty-four

In the morning he saddled up Dusty, his father's old horse, after he finished his morning chores.

Riding into town, he sent Jay on an errand out to Burt Black's while he spent the day getting Harvey's case on paper for Judge Herbert. He wanted to write down what he remembered of the confession before he forgot, while it was still clear in his mind.

He dropped the paperwork off at the Judge's home and went to Edna's for a lunch of potatoes with butter and pork chops with milk gravy.

Just after dark he rode out to Burt Black's chicken farm.

The message he had sent Jay out with was for Burt to shovel the manure out of his chicken coop. Danged if Dan was going to spend the night standing around in two- or three-inch-deep chicken manure.

The smell of the fresh, most recent manure under his feet

would be bad enough, the ammonia smell it created would be uncomfortable.

He rode Dusty into Burt's barn, and putting the old horse in a stall, he nodded a silent greeting to Burt as Burt entered the barn. Taking a small amount of rope from his saddlebag, he stuffed it into his pocket. Burt gave Dusty some oats and fresh water and handed Dan a small three-legged stool used for milking, and an unlit oil lantern. Tonight, Burt omitted jokes about Sarah as he obviously had heard from Jay that Sarah had had a leg accident. Both men spoke only in whispers.

Dan took the stool and lamp and quietly, in the dark, crossed from Burt's barn to the chicken coop, opened the door, and went in. He put the stool against the front wall, where it would be right behind the chicken coop door when it opened, then he sat down on it to wait, the lantern still unlit.

With bad luck he could be spending nights in here for a week or more, until the thief struck again.

Not his favorite place.

Well, at least he had on his oldest clothes and his oldest pair of boots. He, and his boots and clothing, would smell like chicken manure by morning.

The chickens, some of them his own fat, wide-bodied reddish brown chickens, mixed with Burt's slenderer white leghorns, clucked softly. Because it was dark, they couldn't see too well, and so were not alarmed unduly by his presence.

A few clucked annoyance at just the door being opened and closed, but others thought it signaled food and he could hear some getting down off their roosts to explore a bit even in the dark.

The moon rose. Dan could tell only by a few tiny cracks between the planks that made up the chicken coop.

Surrounding Dan's immediate area, except for the place behind the door where Dan's stool was, were chicken roosts, poles attached to the walls at different levels about a foot apart, from floor to ceiling. Most of the chickens spent the night on the roosts.

On two of the other walls were rows and rows of nesting boxes which the chickens went into, hopefully, to lay their eggs. Occasionally a chicken laid one on the floor.

It was a large coop, probably thirty by thirty. Normally holding probably two hundred chickens, it had been depleted by the thief and now held about a hundred and twenty five or so, according to Burt's last count.

Burt was to stay in his house, so that to all outward appearances, things were normal.

Time went by slowly.

Because Dan's back was to the outside wall near the door, he had to be very quiet.

Shortly before midnight, by Dan's reckoning, the door slowly opened.

Moonlight streamed in.

Dan held his breath as the black shape crept in. The first surprise was that the man's shape was not that of a man with a shirt and trousers, but that of a man who held a different kind of job—a politician, or someone like that—the profile in the moonlight was of a man with a frock coat.

The man had no gun out, he had both hands free to catch chickens, and only a cloth sack to put the chickens in, in his hands.

The man came in and shut the door.

Dan let the man feel around in the dark in front of one

of the roosts and put one chicken into the sack. Then he walked over and stood behind the man and put the barrel of his .44 directly in the center of the man's back.

"I'd drop that sack if I were you, and put your hands up, nice and easy."

The chicken thief gave him no resistance.

Dan holstered his gun, tied the thief's hands securely behind his back, and went over and lit the lantern.

It was Horace!

A few seconds later, the door creaked open. Burt started to say, "Saw the lantern go on and . . ."

Burt's eyes widened in amazement.

"Dang! I would have never guessed! Never in a gajillion years! Horace, you dang fool!"

"*Why,* Horace?" Dan asked, his curiosity getting the best of him. "The last thing you need is chickens."

Up until the recent contest, the Zachary family had been feeding Horace all these years.

"Gambling debts—monte," Horace said. He held his head high, nonrepentant, his lower lip drawn up tight over his lower teeth in defiance, his jaw thrust forward in anger.

Burt had recovered enough to joke.

"Well, you want to be in the cell with the killer-for-hire or the crooked banker, Horace? Mebbe Dan, here, will give you yer pick."

He dumped the chicken out of the sack.

"One more question, Horace, what did you do with the chickens?" Burt asked, curious.

"Miners. Sold them to miners." Horace said. "If you people paid me more—"

"That won't wash," Dan reminded him. "You just said it was gambling debts."

Burt said, "I sure am relieved that this was resolved without gunplay."

Then he couldn't resist taunting the ex-teacher. "By the way, Horace, didn't nobody ever *teach* you that being poor ain't no excuse for being dishonest?"

Burt insisted on escorting Horace and Dan back to town and watching Horace get locked up. Dan put him in the cell with Harvey King.

King had been strangely quiet since his arrest, no doubt plotting how he could wiggle out of the charges against him. He made a face, though, at being in a cell with a chicken thief.

"Can't you put him in the other cell?" King demanded. "He stinks!"

"No," Dan said, chuckling. "Besides, he *wants* to be with you."

Horace sat on the one cot, and then laid down.

"He's on *my* cot," King said.

"Then sleep on the floor, Harvey," Burt said, chuckling.

Angrily, King grabbed the blanket, now with chicken manure on it from Horace's boots, from underneath Horace, rolling Horace over. When he smelled the blanket, King threw it on the floor in a rage and went to stand in the farthest corner of the cell.

Later, Dan, sleeping on the cot, had to listen to squabbling almost all night long from the two men. Harvey had managed to get the cot away from Horace and Horace slept on the floor. Jay had given them both clean blankets.

"Shut up!" either Dan, the other prisoner, or Jay had to call out occasionally.

Finally, it was quiet.

In the morning, Dan got up and went outside. It was the beginning of a beautiful sunny day.

Up the street he saw Mrs. Briggs entering Ferd Cody's store with a tiny blue bundle held securely in her arms. Her other two children were beside her, walking close to her.

He ought to be happy to be alive on a day such as this. Maybe, like Charlie, it was time to put the war, and even thoughts of Maryellen, behind him forever.

There was something wonderful about California, he thought, even with its mud and raging summertime rivers, and occasional outlaws. Most of the people were good, solid, honest citizens.

As he stood on the porch outside his office, he saw a wagon drive up and stop outside of Edna's restaurant. He recognized the wagon. It was the wagon of the farmer from Oregon who delivered potatoes to both Edna's Food Emporium and Ferd Cody's general store.

Sitting up there on the wagon seat was the most beautiful woman Dan had ever seen. His stomach did a flip-flop when he saw her. Her thick, curly, reddish-brown hair shone in the sun, and she had on a pretty blue dress. And her skin . . .

She looked over and gave him a wide, friendly smile, and he thought, perhaps she was looking at him with some interest, because it was a long time before she glanced away.

She had to be the woman the pastor kept telling him about.

He thought his heart would bust right out of his chest, it was pounding so hard. And he smelled like chicken manure, and had on his oldest clothes!

He tried to smile back.

Could he possibly rush home and bathe, put on clean clothes, shave, and be back in town before she left?

She smiled at him again, this time, shyly.

He knew he couldn't stand it if he never saw her again.

Then he realized that if she was the daughter of the wagon driver, there was a good chance she would be spending the night in one of the rental rooms up above Edna's restaurant before starting back.

Maybe he could arrange to eat supper at Edna's and get introduced.

Could he be that lucky today?

He thought perhaps he could.